# The Wanting Heart

Rionna Morgan

CRIMSON
ROMANCE
Avon, Massachusetts

This edition published by
Crimson Romance
an imprint of F+W Media, Inc.
10151 Carver Road, Suite 200
Blue Ash, Ohio 45242
*www.crimsonromance.com*

ISBN 10: 1-4405-5168-5
ISBN 13: 978-1-4405-5168-0
eISBN 10: 1-4405-5148-0
eISBN 13: 978-1-4405-5148-2

# Dedication

*A true friend finds a way to celebrate—even in the worst moments of life—and forces it upon you.*

This is for you, my friends, for bringing the coffee, the wine, the chocolate, the lumpy mashed potatoes. Thank you for being everything I needed, even when I didn't know it.

# Acknowledgments

As I sit to type these words, I am in awe. Simply. It seems amazing to me to hold a dream as long as I've held this one and then suddenly in the evening of a spring day, it comes true.

For making this moment possible, I must thank the lovely Jennifer Lawler of Crimson Romance. Thank you also to Terese daly Ramin for finding and suggesting clever ways to weave a bit more into the fabric of this story. A special thank you to Richard Smith, a retired Deputy State Fire Marshal who helped me find a way to blow up a house and hurt no one. Thank you Daniel Robinson for building a beautiful website for me.

A very special thank you the beautiful, talented Kat Martin for always taking the time to be encouraging and helpful, no matter how busy you are.  To The Midnight Writers who have read this book a million times and can still look at me with genuine excitement when I speak of it. To the Montana Romance Writers, you are an amazing group. I feel so very lucky to be counted amongst you. To the members of my writing group—Angie, Danica, Casey, Clare, and Pam—you are wonderful to work with and laugh with. Thank you for always reminding me that *it's good for a rough draft*.

To my children—my son and three daughters—my own personal cheering section. Thank you for taking me seriously even though I often forget to wear shoes. Thank you for supporting me in the best way you know how—writing notes reminding me to do laundry is a good thing. To my husband, thank you for picking up where I leave off. Thank you for the late night kisses of encouragement, the hours of brainstorming and most of all thank you for being the hero of my heart. Above all others I must thank my mother, Margaret E. Whitney, for sharing her everlasting love of words and stories. I miss you, Mom.

And lastly, to my readers. Thank you for pausing for a moment in your busy life to read a story I wrote for you. I hope that Kate, her friends, and Blake entertain you for a while. I love to have visitors, so please be invited to drop by rionnamorgan.com for a chat.

All the Best,
Rionna

# CHAPTER 1

"Hey, Kate."

"Well if it isn't Blake Spencer." Kate finished tightening her horse's cinch. "I didn't know you were here." Which was a lie. She knew because she'd watched his ride. She'd seen him shimmy down into the chute next to a snorting, stomping rodeo bronc. She'd watched him jam his hand into his bareback riggin'. When he was set, he flung his boots high above the shoulder of his ride, leaned back, nodded, and said, "Outside." She knew that all the miles and the lousy coffee and the broken bones found their worth in that first jump. Years ago, she'd heard him call it "rodeo magic." It wasn't just his voice or his eyes or even his body she had loved. It was the valor he showed in the moment where only fear should have been.

"Yeah, I'm here. I scored an eighty-nine on my ride. That'll give me a check. I'm about twelfth in the standings. I don't think that's too bad."

Blake leaned against the side of the horse trailer and watched Kate check Lady's bridle. He cleared his throat. "I want to make it to the Finals. Depending on how my competition does this weekend, I just might."

Kate looked at him and her heart trembled. He looked as easy and comfortable as a honky-tonk hero standing in the doorway of a bar. His dark brown hair waved to the edge of his deep blue eyes. He held his Stetson in his hand. His ridding chaps were gone, probably folded neatly in his gear bag. But his jeans showed the signs of being in the dirt and the left sleeve of his shirt was still rolled to his elbow. He was all cowboy. Other people saw him as the only son of the valley's richest rancher. Kate knew the real man, the kind, gentle one, the funny one, the strong one. She'd known him since high school. They dated then. They traveled the rodeo circuit together. He rode bareback horses. She chased the cans. She'd fallen in love. He'd left.

"What do you want?" Kate asked.

"I want to talk to you."

Kate watched him. He stood perfectly still. His eyes held hers. A slight breeze ruffled his hair and she caught the scent of saddle leather mixed with sweetened spice. Her breath caught. "Damn," she whispered and squeezed her eyes shut.

"I *need* to talk to you." Blake's soothing, drop of whiskey voice murmured.

"About what?"

"I went to Alaska."

"What for?" Kate could hardly stand him being there. The pain was too much to handle.

"That's part of what I wanted to talk to you about. I was hoping that before you drove home, we could grab something to eat and catch up."

"Well, that's easy." Kate's fingers weaved small braids in Lady's mane. "I've been here, going to college, going to rodeos. And you've been gone. I think that about covers it. All caught up." Kate willed herself not to give in to emotion. She'd done enough of that.

"Darlin'." Blake walked to her. "Don't do that. Don't be sad." He smoothed his thumb over her cheek.

The warmth in his hand weakened her. There was a time when she would have gladly closed her eyes and leaned into it. A time when she would have put her arms around him and given what he wanted. But this wasn't one of them.

"Don't call me that." Kate smacked his hand away. "I gotta go." She stepped up into the stirrup. "Come on, Lady Bug." Kate clicked her tongue and pressed her horse forward. Saddle leather creaked as Lady moved with anxious hooves. Kate wished the cowboy behind her wouldn't follow. But she knew that no matter what she did, he would. He was always there, right at the edge of her heart.

*

"It's the fastest horse race on earth, folks. One turn to the right, two to the left—"

The rodeo announcer's voice bellowed from speakers loud enough to be heard above the forever blowing Wyoming wind. The swirling gusts played tag with Lady's silver-gray mane and brushed the chilly March air across Kate's face, as she coaxed Lady to lope a few figure eights to get their blood pumping. The rodeo arena stretching out before them had turned gold in the setting sun. In the twilight Kate saw the clover-leaf pattern she and Lady would run.

The spectators huddled around their thermoses of coffee and each other, needing that extra warmth. It wasn't exactly cold, but Kate knew she needed the long sleeved silk shirt she wore under her sequined one for the added insulation. Many girls wrapped their jackets closer to their chin, but Kate felt like she had a responsibility as an entertainer, and that people paid good money to see the beauty in rodeo. The rhinestones and the sequins in her wardrobe were for them.

Coming to rest beneath the flickering lights that would soon shine as bright as twenty suns, Kate bowed her head and cleared her mind. This was a time of silence for her, when the breeze pulsed in rhythm with her heart. It was almost like the wind swiped the sound of the crowd, and it was just her and Lady, her beloved partner. They had traveled all the miles together over the years. They'd bled. They'd lost. They'd won. Together.

Many nights when Kate couldn't sleep, she'd go to the stables where Lady was. She'd talk to her and Lady would listen with her big gray, understanding eyes. Sometimes it was silly chatter about college or dreams or the girls, but lately it had been sadness that had driven Kate to the stables at midnight. She'd unlatch the gate into Lady's stall and wrap her arms around her neck. Feeling the warmth and strength in it, Kate would sob and ache for all the things she missed. But soon Lady's easy breathing, patience, and the aroma of her sweet mix grain would ease Kate's mind. And she could live through another day without Blake and without her mom. The tears would stop, and together, they'd look forward to the next rodeo.

Kate and Lady had pulled into the out-of-the-way rodeo arena in Wyoming earlier that day to make a walk through. It wasn't so much the town Kate was interested in, but the arena. This dirt was good. It had a sturdy base and enough top to make the slide around the barrels. Kate was thankful. She'd been in worse. Last year was a hard one for luck. It seemed like at every other rodeo, the dirt was either rain-slicked mud or cracked and sunbaked. But that hadn't kept her from being second at the NFR.

This year her sights were set on the World Champion gold buckle that could only be won at the National Finals Rodeo in Las Vegas. It had been her dream for as long as she could remember. She'd started out this year great with the big win at the Stock Show in Denver. Her first place in the standings still held. She knew everything about the girls she competed with today. There were some who traveled the same Mountain States circuit as she did and some that traveled others, but Kate still knew their money earnings, their horses and their hometowns.

Right now, even though she knew all of it, that wasn't what she was thinking about. As she twirled the shamrock-green ribbon tied to her saddle horn, her thoughts were on what she loved to do, what she was good at and that the next few perfect seconds would be shared with Lady. That was what was important. And she was up.

Kate pulled her hat tight and stuck her feet deep in the stirrups. Lady Bug, the dappled-gray Quarter horse beneath her, didn't have to be told it was time to go. She was ready.

The first galloped stride inside the arena gate shot adrenalin and power through their bodies. Kate guided Lady to the first turn to the right. She held her body still so Lady could make the turn and looked to the second barrel. It seemed slow and easy in Kate's mind. She used every angle and every second to the fullest. She twisted and leaned and pushed forward. The second barrel done, they raced to the third. Lady's hooves dug into the dirt, making it fly. Her legs devoured the space. The wind created from their speed whipped around them, making them free. After the third turn, they bolted through the hazy dust of the arena back to the gate.

"That's why they call it turn and burn, folks." The rodeo announcer's voice scratched over the loud speaker. "That's Kate White, ladies and gentlemen, a pretty Colorado cowgirl on her horse Lady Bug. They finished that run with a sixteen and five. Sounds like she'll be in the money to me. Up next we have..."

Kate smiled and jumped down. Sixteen point twenty-one seconds was a fast time for this arena, but sixteen point zero five *was* better! She grabbed Lady's neck in a quick hug. "Thanks, Lady Bug." As she walked Lady back to her horse trailer, Kate listened for the next girl's time, glad she didn't see Blake anywhere. Maybe he went home, she thought and chastised herself for being disappointed.

\*

Blake saw her with reins in hand as she and Lady walked back to the trailer. What a picture they made, he thought, the girl with her horse. Her black Wranglers curved up legs that were both short enough and long enough to be just perfect. The sequins in her shirt added their twinkle to the scene and her hair, the long red banner of it, fell in an easy curl down her back. Lady's easy gate matched Kate's as they walked. It was their rhythm. The rhythm that said, "we do this together." He knew there couldn't be one without the other. He could hear her laugh as she greeted other contestants. If he tried, he knew he could catch her scent on the breeze.

He sighed with yearning. It was the same sigh he'd had tonight as he watched while she waited to enter the arena. The world around her was busy with all the behind the scene details of a rodeo. No one stopped to notice that right there in the middle of the dust and the boots and the bulls was the most wonderful girl in the world. It was still mesmerizing to him to hear how the crowd grew quiet when they saw a beautiful girl on a dappled-gray horse, enter the arena. How the rhinestones in her ears glinted in the evening sun. How her hair swished behind her as she whipped around the barrels. His breath caught at how close she came, her knees scraping the edges of those steel cans. And when she finished, the sound of the crowd cheering as she waved. If there were such a thing as the sweetheart of the rodeo, Kate was it, he thought.

"Might as well try again," he told himself as he kicked a clod of dirt and walked in her direction. "That's a great time. The electric eye sure is more accurate than my watch," he said when he got close enough for her to hear him.

Kate was busy unsaddling Lady, but even though Blake was sure she heard him walk up and saw him lean against the horse trailer, she didn't look at him.

So that's how it'll be. Damn, Blake thought. "I'm sorry."

"For what?" Kate asked as she continued what she was doing.

"I just am," Blake paused. He didn't know what to say. Didn't know how he could convince her to really talk to him. So he said the next thing that came into his mind and could've kicked himself for it, "Have you heard from your mom?"

Kate looked at him from across her saddle. "Why do you care?

You left, remember? Nichole and I were standing at the edge of her hospital bed and you just turned around and walked out."

"I just wanted to know." Blake cursed his stupidity. He didn't want to remind her of one of the biggest mistakes of his life.

"Yes, I hear from her, once a week. She calls to see how I'm doing." Kate put her saddle on its rack and slammed the tack door. "I get to tell her I'm fine, doing great in school, that I graduate in a few months, and that I'm first in the standings this week. And I get to hear her wistful voice say how proud she is of me."

The rodeo announcer's voice interrupted Kate.

"You won." Blake smiled.

"I know." Kate turned and walked toward the rodeo office. How come it didn't feel like it?

*

*Somewhere beyond the reach of that Wyoming rodeo arena, he looked down at his beautiful creation. He was a winner too—to himself at least—because after years of longing, he'd finally had the courage to create. Before him was the first of many who would get exactly what they deserved. This one was especially beautiful; she was his first. Her eyes stared out into the bloodstained moonlight. Carved into her skin was the number one. Her hand gripped a single red rose.*

# CHAPTER 2

"What the hell was he doing there?"

"Geez, Erin." Kate scowled. "I don't know. How many times you gonna ask me?"

"Didn't his grandma tell you?"

"No. And I didn't ask."

"Why not?" Erin pressed.

"It's not that big a deal."

"Not that big a deal?" Erin threw up her hands. "Oh, yeah. You're right. You moping for a week and being a royal pain in the ass, is no big deal. What was I thinking? And why didn't you ask her?"

Kate's lips twisted. "Because she'll just try to convince me to give him another chance."

"Oh, yeah." Erin snorted. "That'll work. You haven't even seen him for three years."

Four. "Leona just wants me to be happy." Kate looked at the clothes rack in front of her. She knew the perfect dress for tonight existed. She just had to find it.

"No shit and you think we don't?"

"Of course you, Ranae and Nichole want me to be happy. Leona just doesn't understand that I don't want anything to do with Blake anymore." Kate pushed another dress to the side.

"What the hell's he doing back in Colorado anyway?" Erin couldn't—or *wouldn't*—let it go. "I thought he was in Alaska or something."

"Don't know." Kate loved her friend, but the push-push-push had worn thin several questions ago.

"You haven't heard from him, have you?" Erin stood with her feet planted and her hands on her hips.

Kate gritted her teeth. "Not since the rodeo."

"Good." Erin held up a purple velvet dress with leopard collar and cuffs. "Hey, look at this? Do you think Luke'll like it?"

"God! No, that's awful. I don't know exactly what I'm supposed to wear, but I know *that* is not it." Kate shuddered. "We have to keep searching. This place hasn't let me down yet."

Kate and Erin Wilkes were browsing through clothes racks at My Sister's Closet, a consignment shop that was perfect for the needs of two college girls. The store had an antique quality about it. Old, squeaky dressers were decorated with embroidered doilies under kerosene lanterns. There were tall oval mirrors on swivels. Parasols and lacey gloves adorned the shelves and any other nook available. On one of the shelves there were even some old time shoes that nobody could ever have had feet small enough to fit in. The whole store was a picture to behold, but the real gold mine was in the clothes.

Kate couldn't believe she was shopping for a dress to go on a real Friday night date with a guy who wasn't Blake Spencer, the only guy she'd ever dated. Ever loved. In fact she'd only known Luke for a few days. They'd met five days ago at the The Pub with Erin, Ranae, and Nichole. Even now, when Kate thought of their meeting, she shook her head at how unbelievable it was. She and the girls had finished their first toast of the evening, celebrating Nichole's visit, and when she looked up, she saw him.

Luke Ferral—exotic like James Bond. He was completely comfortable in the black tuxedo he wore. The jacket hung open, several of the buttons on the shirt were free and the collar was flipped up. One hand was in his pocket and the other held a tumbler of dark liquid and ice. He was completely out of place with all the t-shirts and blue jeans around, but he just stood near the girls' table lounging against the wall like The Pub couldn't have existed without him. Black curly hair fell almost to his eyes. Oh, and what eyes, they were a dusky midnight. His gaze held hers. Captivated her. When Kate tried to look away, those midnight eyes followed. She tried to speak. When she stumbled over her words, an easy grin touched his lips. He walked straight to her and took her hand in his. If the tux hadn't been enough to prove that he wasn't from around here, his hand was. It was smooth. Surprised, Kate blinked. Luke kissed her hand and knelt before her.

"I'm Luke."

Again Kate tried to say something. She tried to stand. She tried—something.

"She's Kate," Ranae said for her.

"I'm sure she's really glad to meet you." Nichole grinned.

"If not, I sure the hell am," Erin said.

"Shut up." Ranae elbowed Erin.

"Well, she's not saying shit." Erin pouted.

"She doesn't have to talk, maybe she'll dance?" Luke said as he pulled Kate out of her chair.

Kate nodded and followed Luke to the dance floor.

He twirled her once, drew her close and let her fall into a dip so low her hair brushed the floor. Kate blinked and smiled at the romance of it.

"There now, that wasn't so hard." Luke looked into her eyes and grinned.

"No, I guess not." Kate nodded.

They laughed and spent the rest of the evening together. The girls loved it. Luke brought flowers the next day to the college office where Kate worked. Each day after, there were always flowers: tulips, lilacs, daisies, orchids. They had gone for walks in the park and eaten ice cream at the river, but tonight was their first real date.

"Maybe this will work." Kate looked at a peach blouse with a bit of lace at the collar. "There are only so many places we can go in this town and if I wear a nice black skirt…"

"Yeah, I guess." Erin nodded. "But I wish we could find *the* dress." Still not satisfied, she continued to paw her way through the racks. "Hey, why don't you go ask the woman up front—oh no wait, look!" Erin held up a beautiful ivory dress. "It looks like satin. If we could find a wrap to go, it would be perfect."

Kate ran her hand over the fabric. "It's pretty."

"Go try it on and I'll try to find a wrap and some shoes—and some jewelry, and maybe a hat or something else that might work. We don't have to use it all, but it never hurts to be prepared." Erin pushed Kate toward the dressing room.

Half an hour later Kate and Erin were loaded down with flimsy gray plastic bags holding Kate's treasures for the night. The wrap was found and shoes were decided on. With just two hours to go before the date, Kate and Erin rushed to the apartment where Ranae and Nichole waited to do hair and make-up and give orders.

Kate was excited, when she walked through the door to the apartment with Erin close behind.

"Kate, oh-my-gosh, you have got to see this package that just arrived for you." Ranae raced to the door and pulled Kate to her room.

On her bed sat a huge white box with a single red envelope attached that stated: *From Luke.* Kate didn't waste any time tearing into the envelope. In neat small handwriting Kate read, *I saw this today and thought of you. This holds a beauty only you can match. Your magic green eyes, your hair lit with sunset will make the perfect union with this. Please, it will honor me if you wear it. Luke*

Giddy shrieks of delight rang through the apartment as the girls danced in circles around Kate.

"That's so romantic," yelled Nichole.

"Well, open it, we have to see it!" Erin grabbed the box and began pulling off the lid. All the girls helped. Ripping the box, throwing the tissue paper, but when they reached the gift inside, they stopped in silent shock.

"It's so beautiful," Kate said in a reverent tone as she pulled the gown from the box. "It's the perfect dress."

"No shit," said Erin.

"Oh, please wear it—it goes with these shoes and you have to wear them." Nichole held out the shoes that had been just beneath the next layer of tissue paper.

"Oh my!" Kate reached for the shoes. They felt like nothing they were so light. The same pattern of jewels that decorated the bodice of the gown adorned the toe of the shoe. The rest, which was little, felt of satin and had a single thin strap to keep it on.

"They match exactly. Isn't that awesome," Ranae said feeling a bit like a country bumpkin because she had only read about such beautiful clothing.

"They kind of look like ballet slippers with a heel." Nichole pointed at the shoes.

"Oh yeah and you would know wouldn't you, Hollywood." Erin grinned with her hands clasped under her chin not caring that she had a mushy look on her face and added. "Well you'd better start putting that on so you can go on your date in this big fancy town. Where are you going to anyway?"

"I don't know. We'd talked about going to the new steak house on the edge of town where they let you cook your own steak." Kate secretly hoped they wouldn't now that she was wearing this dress. She knew she would probably have to give it back, and she didn't want to accidentally get a stain on it.

"The Angus? I heard their steak is really good," Ranae said.

"Well, big damn deal. How's she going to cook a steak in that dress?" Erin flicked her fingers at the dress.

"She'll worry about that when the time comes, but Erin's right, we had better get going. You want me to do your hair or—?" Nichole stopped when the phone rang.

"I'll do her hair, you answer that damn thing," directed Erin, "and you two can do the gunk on her face."

"I need to take a quick shower, first." Kate ran to bathroom stripping out of her clothes as she went. I can't believe this, what an adventure, thought Kate as she lathered her hair.

Caught up in the romance of the moment, it didn't once occur to her to think it strange that Luke had known exactly what size dress and shoes she wore...

*

The adventure was getting old and she hadn't even seen Luke yet. She was too busy sitting on a chair in the middle of her bathroom while Nichole, Erin, and Ranae said, *move your head, stop moving, open your eyes, close your eyes, open your mouth, close your mouth.* She'd had just about enough.

"I have never had so much stuff in my hair or had it up so many different ways in so short a time," she exclaimed finally. "Worse, I'm going to look like a rodeo clown with all the make-up."

"Well do you want to look elegant or do you want to look like some dumb little inexperienced nobody?" Erin spun the next curl.

"Elegant, of course."

"Then shut up and just sit there."

"Well, can I at least see what you are doing?"

"No!" yelled Ranae and Nichole. They were applying the finishing touches to Kate's eye make-up.

"Fine. Then who was on the phone?"

Nichole looked at the other girls, wishing that she didn't have to say anything. "Blake."

"What? What did he say?"

"That he wanted to talk to you." Nichole reached for Kate's hand.

"Yeah. I've heard that. What'd you tell him?"

"That you were just leaving for a date?"

"What! Then what'd he say? Never mind. I don't want to know." Kate squeezed Nichole's hand.

"Who wants to know what that asshole wanted anyway?" Erin muttered under her breath.

"Let's not talk about him. I want to finish getting Kate ready," Ranae said.

"I wish I didn't have to go back to L.A. tomorrow." Nichole added powder to Kate's cheek. "But I'll send a web cam so you guys can send live footage of their next date."

"If there is one," Kate amended.

"If there is one?" Ranae shook her head.

"A guy doesn't spend all this money for one date," Erin said. "The web cam's a good idea. My business teacher uses one all the time. I think I'm about done here." Erin sprayed the final curl with hairspray.

"We're done, too." Nichole put the fat powder brush back in the make-up tub.

"Finally." Kate stood and turned to look in the huge vanity over the sink. "Wow! I've never looked this good in my whole life and I'm still in my bathrobe." Her strawberry red curls were pinned up and made to look like a crown of fire. Fastened at every curl was an emerald jewel that Erin had taken off of the wrap that would no longer be used. Her hair looked like a fireball with winking green stars. "Erin, it's beautiful." Kate turned to hug her friend.

"Don't touch me with your head. I'm not doing any fixing," Erin grouched, but smiled and hugged her back. "Thanks, it's beautiful. And no crying, we don't have time to re-apply your war paint."

War paint indeed! Her whole face shimmered. A delicate green graced her eyelids as a darker green lined the edges. Her cheeks were bronze with borrowed fire and her lips were glossed with a touch of red.

"We wanted your eyes to be the focus. When you put on the gown the red gloss will be plenty, but the green of your eyes, whew! Luke will be speechless." Nichole tapped her lips.

"Let's go put on your dress." Ranae moved toward the door.

"Nae, I'm so excited." Butterflies fluttered in Kate's stomach. "I wish we had a more elegant place to go, but I don't care even if we have to cook our own steak."

"Well, maybe you'll drive to Denver or somewhere. They have better places there."

"Maybe. I never thought of that. I don't know why not, though. Mom and I would think nothing of jumping in the truck and heading for Cheyenne for ice cream." Kate smiled, laid her bathrobe on the bed and bent into the dress when Ranae lifted it over her head. "Mom would just wake me up in the morning and say, let's do the chores and go have ice cream for breakfast. Of course we'd be starving by the time we left, because it took hours to actually get out of town. I always had a banana split if we went to Cheyenne, but sometimes we would go to this tiny town in Kansas—Winthrop?— heck, I can't remember. But they had the best brownie hot fudge sundae ever. I'd forgotten all about that." Kate looked at Ranae. "Maybe next weekend we could go have ice cream in Cheyenne."

"Why not. That sounds like the perfect breakfast," Ranae agreed, knowing how much Kate missed her mother.

"Why don't you talk to Erin about it and—" The doorbell rang. "Holy crap, is it time already? I need earrings or something."

"Kate, you're fine. You look beautiful. Now stop being so nervous. I'll talk to Erin about ice cream and you just have fun." Ranae reached to hug Kate. "I love you."

"I love you, too." Kate hugged her back. "And I am going to have a great time! That I promise you."

With that, Kate turned and walked down the short hallway to the living room, feeling a little like Cinderella going to the ball.

Luke was seated and looking as nonchalant as ever in another tux, but there was something different about his eyes. They looked stunned or maybe awed or both. Kate just smiled hoping that he would like the way she looked. When he tried to speak, she laughed.

"He's speechless," Nichole laughed too.

But Luke was not motionless. He strolled to Kate and knelt before her, held her hand and kissed it. Turning her hand over, he placed a tiny box on her palm. Around her Kate could hear her friends draw in a fast breath at the same time Kate drew in hers. Luke opened the lid of the box and lying on a bed of white velvet were two emerald earrings. A small diamond sat at the top while the emerald dripped into a tear. Luke stood and fastened the ring to each ear. Then he stepped back.

"In all my dreams I have searched for you and here you stand. My Irish goddess. Beauty that walks and laughs and dances." He pulled Kate in a twirl and then let her fall into a long slow dip held strong by his one arm. The other hand caressed her cheek. "Thank you for sharing a few moments of your life with me."

"You're welcome." Kate smiled. "And thank you, the gown is beautiful."

"Is it? I hadn't noticed." Luke's midnight eyes swam with Kate's as his lips gently touched her cheek.

\*

*For him, there'd been one other red-head. So very special. Yet, he was alone. Confused. His mother had left him. He searched his memories. Somewhere within them he heard pleading. Why had she gone? He took comfort in the arms of women—their hearts bled for him. And when he was finished with them, he placed only a rose on the altar of their bodies.*

# CHAPTER 3

*What luxury*, thought Kate as she slid her hand over the toffee colored seat beneath her. *I'm sitting in a limousine!* The leather was so smooth and supple it felt like the way chocolate mousse should taste. The girls are going to love it. She tried to suppress a snicker, but didn't quite manage.

"Is something funny?" Luke slid closer to her.

"No, not at all. I just can't get over the beauty of the evening. The girls are going to be so envious."

"Well let's give them something else to envy." Luke handed her a slim flute of champagne shimmering with golden bubbles.

"Is this a dream? I keep asking myself if it is." Kate took a sip. "I'm not going to ask you to pinch me or anything, but there's got to be some test."

"I think there just might be."

Luke pulled Kate to him. She felt a small kiss on her shoulder blade just above the neckline of the dress. A small thrill traveled through her body. She felt hypnotized, drugged. Closing her eyes, she focused on the sensations that made it feel as though her blood floated through her veins. The kiss, the caress followed the curve of her neck, stopping before it reached her lips.

"Are you dreaming?" Luke's lazy voice flirted with her senses.

"Yes, definitely." Kate smiled, trying to act sophisticated as she took a large drink of the bubbling liquid. She knew Luke wasn't from here. He couldn't be. He was from somewhere where people dressed in tuxes and rode in limousines and dated sophisticated women. Which she was not, but it would be fun to feel the part for even a short time. She loved the little sporadic surprises he'd offered her all week. The flowers at work, the ice cream at the river, the gown for this evening's dinner and the limousine ride. Luke made her feel free. She didn't have to worry so much about the life she faced for real. No cares, just laughter and fun—a perfect evening to the perfect day.

He laughed. It was a smooth laugh—cozy and warm like a fire in a log cabin covered with snow. "What do you like to eat?"

"I like steak." Kate thought of the new little restaurant on the edge of town. Hoping her last hope that they weren't going there, but being resigned to it if they were, she finished the drink in her glass, which Luke immediately refilled.

"What else do you like to eat? I'm not quite sure they have steak where we're going tonight."

*Oh good, I won't have to worry about cooking my own food*, Kate thought at she took another drink. "I like fish. I'm not big on chicken." Would a sophisticated girl say that? Not likely. "Rather, I am not fond of chicken."

"What else?"

What else is there? Spaghetti, yuck. Lasagna, so-so. Pizza, good. "I like pizza."

"If you don't mind, perhaps you will let me order for you tonight?"

"Yes, of course." I can stand anything really, Kate thought as she sipped from her glass again. She enjoyed the bubbly sweet taste. Chilled at the edges it was almost ice. Kate took another drink. "Where are we going?" Kate tried hard to stifle a yawn. "Sorry, I was up almost all of last night trying to take a picture of the moon that would turn out better."

"Better than what?" Luke asked.

"Better than the last million I've taken." Kate smiled through sleepy eyes.

"Why are you taking a picture of the moon?"

"It's for my photography class at school."

"I thought you were going to be a teacher?"

"I am. I just like taking pictures." Kate yawned again. "Sorry."

"It's fine. Why don't you rest? We have quite a distance to go."

"Where are we going?" Kate asked again, but could barely keep her eyes open. She finished her drink and handed the flute to Luke afraid she might drop it.

"It'll be a surprise."

Kate hardly heard Luke's response. Her eyes were closed and she was dreaming a dream she'd had many times before. She dreamt she was riding her barrel horse Lady Bug in a smooth, rhythmic gallop. She and Blake were gathering cows. Blake was astride his huge bay gelding. Side by side they rode, hand in hand. Smiling, Blake was telling her of the dreams he had about owning his own ranch. It would be something bigger and far grander than what there was in Colorado. "We could go to Wyoming or Montana," he said. "They have rodeos there and miles of grassland with mysterious coulees. There are rivers so wide and crystal clear that it seems the glaciers they come from have just begun to melt. Kate, I want you to be there with me."

Then something pulled their hands apart. He was riding away to the hill beyond. He didn't look back.

"No, wait. Don't leave again!" Kate cried in her dream. Why did he always have to go? Why couldn't he just stay and work for the dreams he spoke of? Why? Come back.

"Katherine," a voice called from the edge of her dream. "Katherine." A hand smoothed her face.

"Blake," Kate whispered.

"You were having a bad dream."

"Why do you always leave?"

"I'm right here."

"I'm so glad." Kate's arms reached for the voice. "I'm so glad."

"Are you hungry?" the voice asked.

"Luke?"

"That must've been some dream."

"Yeah it was."

"Do you want to tell me about it?"

"Not really, it's just sad and I don't want to be sad tonight." Kate sat up. She noticed that they weren't in the limo anymore. She was lying on a bed. "Where am I?" Kate asked. She tried to keep the fear from her voice.

"We're on my plane."

"You have a plane? With a bed—where are we?" Kate looked down at the soft red blanket covering her. "How long did I sleep? Where are we going?" Kate knew anger was evident in her words. "Why didn't you tell me where we were going? How did I get here?"

"I carried you. You slept about two hours and I did tell you—remember I said it was going to be a surprise?" Luke smiled. "I didn't do any of this to upset you. I truly wanted it to be a surprise, but you were still sleeping when we got to the airstrip, and I didn't want to wake you."

Kate could see the beginnings of hurt in his eyes and felt bad.

"We have just landed in San Francisco and we can go eat now."

"San Francisco, California?"

"Do you think the girls will be envious of this?" Luke smiled again.

"Wait. We flew to San Francisco to have dinner?"

"I thought you might like to see the sunset over the bay and eat a nice meal."

"The *San Francisco* Bay?"

"Yes, that's where we are." Luke smiled and paused. "And if you keep repeating everything I say, we'll miss the sunset."

"Okay. Sorry. I just can't believe we're doing this. It's like something my mother would do." A few tears slipped down Kate's cheek. "She would think nothing of it. Let's feed the horses early and eat dinner in California." Kate shook her head.

Luke smoothed the tears away. "Let's not be sad. I wanted you to have a lovely evening. Perhaps we'll bring your mother next time. Maybe she'd like to ride horses on the beach."

"She can't."

"Why not?" Luke held her hand.

"She had a heart attack almost five years ago and isn't able to do much."

"Where does she live?"

"Oregon."

"Why?"

"She chose Oregon because it was one of the places she'd never lived and because it has a lower elevation than Colorado." Kate chuckled remembering when her mom chose Oregon from the list of states with lower elevations the doctor gave her.

"She sounds adventurous." Luke smiled.

"She is."

"Well, we'll think about something she can do with us and since you have..." Luke paused. "A barrel run next weekend?"

Kate nodded and smiled at Luke's effort to use the correct term.

"Maybe we'll take her the weekend after."

"She'd love that."

She shouldn't have been, but Kate was surprised that Luke had a whole room reserved just for them. The only table in the room was set off center and was graced with a long shear white cloth. Surrounding the room were tall candelabras holding many slender white tapers. Their flame spoke of romance and of welcome. From the ceiling hung three chandeliers with the same white candles. The whole room smelled of wild roses picked at their sweetest. Somewhere unseen, a violin hummed a graceful melody.

"I can't believe it. I know for sure I'm dreaming," Kate whispered. "Places like this don't really exist."

"Yes they do, I made it for you." Luke pulled Kate to the sliding door. "And we made it just in time." Opening it, he let in the world of the California ocean. Salt, laughter, warmth and tanning oil permeated the air. Suspended above the beach, they stood on a balcony. The March sky was drenched in reds. Scarlet burned in the sun's trail. Deep blood red touched the water. The clouds that had been white in the day were now diamonds melting with a ruby's blush. The sun bewitched the horizon as it slipped by to begin another day on the other side.

"Thank you, Luke. It's a beautiful sunset." A breeze scented with coconut oil tickled the curled tendrils of Kate's hair.

"You'll have to thank someone else for that. I had nothing to do with it. I, personally, would have made it last longer. So I could enjoy it more." Holding Kate's hand, Luke walked back in the room. "I ordered our dinner on the plane." Luke nodded to the waiter standing by. "This is baked brie with toasted almonds and dried cranberries."

"Sounds lovely," Kate replied as Luke helped her into her seat.

The meal was a wonder. There were tastes and textures Kate had never experienced. The brie was as warm and creamy as the bread she ate with it was moist and flaky. For the main course Luke ordered a salmon fillet with tomato relish. The platter itself was beautiful. The red of the tomato lavished the pink-peach salmon. The salad, Luke said, had six different types of lettuce. Imagine. With imported olives, marinated baby tomatoes and a honey-mustard tarragon dressing. But the dessert! Never before had Kate tasted anything so amazing. It was food from Mount Olympus, had to be. In swirls of mandarin orange cream there was passion fruit wrapped in delicate almond cake—a masterpiece of dessert.

"I've gone from one wow tonight to another." Kate looked up to find Luke's eyes searching her face. "The evening was beautiful. I don't really know how to thank you. This is the grandest date I've ever been on."

"You have thanked me."

"I know, but I'm not used to this." Kate didn't really know how to describe the romance and excitement of the whole evening. "It is extravagant."

"I think you are worth a little extravagance—don't you?"

"This doesn't even compare with anything I've ever known. I grew up on a ranch in the mountains of Colorado. I'm a barrel racer. I live in a town with three stoplights. If I say I'm worth a little extravagance—to me that's saying I'm worth a nice steak, a bouquet of roses, a romantic movie and little dancing to end the night. This," Kate spread her arms to encompass the whole room, "is something I would not say I deserved." She paused. "But I've truly enjoyed."

"Hmmm. There is no steak. No movie, no roses, not tonight. But the dancing, I think we can manage." Again Luke nodded to the waiter. Instantly, a violin began a soft rhythm that Kate recognized as an Irish tune she liked.

"The Briar and the Rose," she said as Luke held her body to his, almost touching, and circled her about him enough to make the skirt of her gown flair. It made her feel very elegant and very beautiful.

"Yes, I thought you might enjoy it. It was playing the first night we met, and I danced with you."

"I don't even remember that."

"I have a keen memory. I remember many things that others consider odd or even silly."

"Like what?"

"Like how you looked tonight as you watched the sun go down. I know you've seen sunsets before, but I don't think I'll ever forget the awe with which you watched this one. It was striking and very alluring."

"I don't think that's silly or odd to remember my face. It's nice." Kate felt sad for him. Like somewhere in his life someone must have ridiculed him. She deepened her smile, letting her eyes shine with it.

"Thank you."

Luke pulled Kate closer. The shoes she wore made her tall enough so that her eyes were almost even with his. Each time she looked into them she felt like there was only him in the world. It was like he could reach in her mind and read her thoughts.

Luke's hands moved up and down her back in a slow easy pattern. His lips again moved to the neckline of her gown and slowly kissed their way up almost to her lips. Pausing briefly, he twirled Kate so her back was against his chest. His arms wound around her waist. His lips caressed a trail of warmth from her right shoulder blade to where her hair met her neck. He made the same trail again from her left shoulder blade up. Kate's body responded with warmth in return. She leaned back against him and enjoyed his soft breath on her skin.

"Do you want to stay?" Luke asked.

"Mmm?"

"Do you want to stay here in San Francisco? I've reserved two rooms for us." Luke paused. "I've arranged for our clothing for tonight and tomorrow to be taken to the hotel. I thought we could go parasailing or something fun tomorrow and then fly back or we could go home tonight. Whatever you want to do."

"I'd need to call Ranae."

Luke smiled, reached around to his back and pulled out a tiny phone. "I have my phone right here."

*

*This time in California the man's dark eyes glared into the terrified eyes of the girl beneath him. Ramming himself into her, he slammed the knife's sharp blade to her heart. Carving a six, leaving a rose, he smiled, too.*

# CHAPTER 4

Blake loved early morning on the ranch. As he left the house, the screen door slammed behind him. He winced. He knew Grandma would tell him about it, when he went back in for breakfast. But he wasn't concerned about Grandma's scoldings now. He was more interested in how the air felt cleaner this time of day. It smelled fresher, like the light of the moon had washed it. The rising sun made the out buildings stand taller. The red of the barn shone brighter in the striking light. While the new warmth of the day struggled to overcome the chilly morning, the hot cup of coffee in his hand warmed his insides and steamed into the frosty March air.

His long shadow followed his steps when his boots crunched through the top layer of frozen snow. When he was younger, Blake often wished his shadow could talk. Being raised mainly by his grandparents, he didn't see his parents or sisters much. They lived in town, but Blake loved the ranch. When Grandpa was really busy, Blake had spent many a lonely day wishing for someone to play with. Out here he was an only child and some days he'd wished for a friend. His shadow was always there. It seemed likely to his seven-year-old self that a shadow might be able to talk. But it didn't.

A friend never really came until Kate. She knew when he was sad or happy or even when he needed someone to talk to or at least she used to. She used to come by to see if there was anything she could do to help. She'd pull up in that long horse trailer of hers and unload Lady Bug. She'd zip around saddling Lady and across the pastures they'd fly. It seemed to Blake sometimes that together, Kate and Lady had wings.

Looking out across the pasture now, he could almost feel the beat of Lady's hooves on the turf. He could see her breath in the frozen morning air. Kate's long red hair stretched behind her like a banner of freedom. If he concentrated, Blake could feel Kate's eyes fill with…elation was the only word for it. Oh! How he missed her expressive eyes. The green of them was so piercing it shot to his soul. Kate's laughter was contagious and it started in her eyes.

An ache of misery filled his heart.

Blindly, Blake traveled to the chicken yard and threw in a handful of oats knowing that Grandma would be out later with the scraps and to gather the eggs. He saw to the steers, the few sheep and hogs then stopped to spend some time with the horses. He began to focus on the job at hand. Even though cows made the money for the ranch, horses were the heart of it. They were the oil that made the machine run. Years ago Grandpa decided to try snowmobiles to round up cows in the winter, and he even bought a couple four-wheelers for the spring. But they broke down and the horses came back out. Grandpa just laughed at the other ranchers who had problems with their "gas powered demons" as he called them.

The quick click of the gate latch startled a special silver-gray horse. The small filly nickered to him as he shuffled across the corral. Seeing her deep gray, kind eyes, he thought of Kate's Lady Bug.

This little gray horse was just about a year old. The small filly was of the same bloodlines as Kate's horse. They were full sisters in fact and were almost identical in appearance. Blake called her Little Lady for now. But when I give her to Kate she'll name her, Blake thought. He'd worked for hours with Little Lady. She could now be led with a halter and even jumped into the trailer. All she needed was a barrel racer to learn a little more. All she needed was Kate. Leaning against the pole fence, Blake thought of his plan. He'd gone to Alaska to earn money, partly so he could buy Little Lady. Lady Bug, Kate's horse, would soon be eleven years old. By the time Little Lady was ready for real competition, Lady Bug would be ready for retirement. He just needed to convince Kate to at least talk to him about everything so that he could give Little Lady to her. It'd be easier if he could undo what he'd done. But he couldn't. And to make it harder he had to hear about how she was busy going on dates. Who the hell with, he wondered. And why wasn't she home yesterday when I called?

"Hey, kid! What're you doing? Watching that horse grow?" called a strong voice from the gate.

"Hi, Grandpa." Blake smiled and turned to see his hero, Jack Blake Spencer. Blake had seen him do things with a rope, a cow and a horse that the best rodeo stunt show couldn't match. And he'd done it all in a day's work. But Jack was getting older. He'd pretty much given the ranch management over to Blake. In Blake's opinion, the highlight of Jack's week now was to go to coffee. Sunday, he said, was a great day to get coffee, no church needed for him. "Hell, I get enough church. I live with your grandma don't I? I want some swearing once in a while." And so he goes on Sunday, probably just to drive her crazy.

"Grandma says you had better get your fanny inside if you want breakfast or she's throwing it to the crows," laughed Jack.

"Yeah. Just give me a minute. I need to finish the feeding."

"Suit yourself, but don't be surprised if you have to rustle your own meal. It will be cold cereal for you, buddy." Jack walked back to the house.

Right, Blake thought. It'd be a million years before Grandma would let him have cold cereal in her kitchen. He could hear her now. "As long as I am alive and able to stir the pot, you will eat a hot meal. I don't care how much of a hurry you say you're in." Boy, and was that right. Blake had missed the bus too many times to remember because he'd been eating a hot meal.

"Hey, Little Lady. How you holdin' up?" whispered Blake. "Pretty soon, I'm going to introduce you to your new owner."

Little Lady twitched an ear as if understanding.

"Yup. That's right, the barrel racer. Pretty soon. Pretty soon. Have a good day, little one. I'll see you tonight." Blake smoothed her mane and laughed at her blinking at him as he clicked the gate in place.

This time Blake made sure the screen door didn't slam as he went in. Grandma Leona and Grandpa were having quite the discussion when Blake sat at the table after washing up.

"Well, I told you that guy was no good as a ditch rider," Leona said tartly.

"Yes. I know it. I didn't vote for him."

"Steve's a drunk and you know it."

"Damn it woman, don't you listen? Norman called when he got there to say he saw some fence down on the north end. And that Steve's truck was parked right in the middle of it. I thought I should drive in and see what all the fuss was about." Jack scowled at Blake's suppressed laugh.

Blake would have gotten cuffed, if Grandpa knew what Blake had been thinking. He and Grandma sounded like a woman running to the hair salon to get the latest gossip.

"Well, why didn't you say so?" Leona stood with her hands on her hips.

"That's what I have been saying, woman."

"You should go check on it!"

"Good idea." Jack laughed. He was used to this kind of fighting with Leona. It was what had made him fall in love with her fifty years ago. Sometimes, he told Blake wistfully, he wished that she'd start to get old and her fire wouldn't burn so hot. But Leona's dark blue eyes still snapped and her tongue was still true. And he still loved her for it. Smiling, he looked up at her.

"What are you ogling, you old goat?" snapped Leona, laughter dancing in her eyes.

"Just you, darlin'. Just you."

"Well, if you two are done fightin' I'll be havin' my breakfast," Blake intervened.

"You'll be having your breakfast on your head if'n you're not careful. And you be sure to watch the door, boy. We only have so many hinges." Leona served heaping spoons of hash browns and eggs with bacon and toast.

"Kid, what are you up to today?" Jack asked.

"Those two heifers still haven't calved after last week's branding. I thought I'd go to the south end and check on them." When he was younger it had bothered him to be called kid, but he hardly noticed anymore. Only when it was a serious matter did Blake hear his given name.

"Sounds good. I'm going to run over and check the downed fences like Leona suggested." He nodded his head toward Leona and winked at Blake. "When you're done, why don't you come on over and we'll see what we can do."

"I'd like to ride today, if that's okay." Blake had some things he wanted to sort out and thinking was always better on the back of a horse.

"Sure enough. I'll take the flat-bed."

As Blake ate, his eyes wandered. The white kitchen walls were simple, but Grandma's hand sewn curtains touched them with home. Silver pots of all sizes hung from the frame he and Grandpa had fastened to the ceiling last summer. Leona was not quite five foot so it had to be hung low. Blake and Grandpa at over six foot were forever hitting their heads on the bean pot and swearing, but Grandma loved it. So it stayed. What a home they had made for a lonely little boy. Angry words were never spoken here, perhaps a few cross ones, but bitterness, never. In Blake's opinion, love was felt here like no other place on earth.

"Thanks for breakfast, Grandma," Blake put his dishes in the sink and kissed her cheek. "I'll see you at lunch. Do you need anything from outside before I go?"

"Nope. Sure don't. I'll be out and about soon. Thought I'd go into town and buy a new pair of boots."

"Lord, woman, what the hell do you need a new pair of boots for? You have thirty of 'em stacked in the closet as it is," hollered Jack.

"What are you yelling about? Besides I said I thought. Doesn't mean I will!"

Before Blake got cornered into saying something, he headed out. He shut the screen door lightly, hoping they wouldn't notice. About twenty feet away he could still hear them hackling. *Doesn't mean I will.* Whew. Yes it does, he thought. They'd probably be red. Grandma loved red.

*

"Would you stop shouting for a minute?" gripped Leona after she was certain Blake was gone. "And listen. I wanted Blake to skedaddle so I could talk to you, alone."

"About what?"

"Kate."

"What about her?"

"Blake's got a burr under his saddle about her. That's what."

"How do you know?"

"Well, you heard him say that he wanted to ride. That always means he's got some thinking to do. And Kate is what he's thinking about. I know 'cause I saw a letter to her on his dresser this morning."

"Did you read it?"

"Oh, for heavens sake. No, I didn't read it!"

"Why not?"

"It's none of my business."

"Oh. Horse shit. If you wanted to, you would have read it."

"Well I didn't. But, I got an idea on how to help 'em out."

Jack didn't necessarily like the look in Leona's eye. "What's your idea?"

"For you to talk to him. Tell him how it is with men and women."

"And how is it?" Jack's eyes joked.

"You know."

"I do?" He shook his head

"Yes." Leona whacked him on the back of the head with a potholder. "Would you just talk to him?"

"Yes, dear. I'll talk to him," Jack crossed to the door, not having a clue as to what to say to Blake.

Leona followed.

"I'll see you this afternoon. I think you ought to get some boots. Make 'em red." Jack winked. "I love you." Jack leaned down to kiss her.

"I love you too, old man." She stood on tip-toe and kissed him back. Smiling all the while inside knowing exactly what color of boots she was going to buy—red, white, and blue. They'd be wonderful! She could hardly wait.

*

The sun was about halfway up the horizon when Blake arrived at the pasture. He saw right away that one of the calves had been born. Just at the edge of the feeding pen in the shelter of the fence a little red and white face peered at him. The little feller stood up on wobbly legs and struggled slowly to his mother's side. Watching them made Blake smile. It sure was nice to see a miracle once in a while.

Not wanting to bother the new calf too much Blake turned about to search for the other heifer. She was moving slow, but looked like it would be another day or two. All was well here so he headed to the north pasture at a quick gallop. *Need Kate, need Kate* resounded with the beat of his pulse and his horse's pounding hooves all the way there. How? *How?* Was the question Blake kept asking.

"Hey, kid," Grandpa called when he arrived.

"Hey, Grandpa."

"Damn! That Steve character sure made a hell of a mess!" Jack wiped his sleeve across his brow.

"You've been working hard for a while. Let me have a go." Blake took the wire cutters and barbed wire from Jack's hands.

"Well, what the hell am I supposed to do?" Jack grouched more to himself than to Blake.

It was hell getting old.

"How was the talk at coffee this morning," Blake encouraged. Knowing that all Jack needed was a little prompting and he would talk for an hour about a conversation that lasted five minutes in the coffee shop.

"Hell, we didn't do much talking." Jack tried to figure how the devil he was going to do what Leona had ordered. Just say something, he thought. "How's that little pony doing?"

"Little Lady? Oh. She's doing great. She's really smart."

"When are you going to give her to Kate?"

"I don't know."

"You'd better get a move on it."

"I know. It's just she won't listen to me. I tried talking to her."

"Stop trying and do it."

"Easy for you to say."

"Hell, yes it is. How do you think I got the woman I married? Gave her flowers? She'd have thrown them in my face. No sir. I found what her heart wanted and gave her that. Boots! Yes sirree!" Jack nodded, clearly remembering the first pair he'd ever given her. "Now mind you she didn't take to them right away. In fact she hated them. I got those in my face. Wrong color. Next pair. They were red. Now that was the winner."

"Kate doesn't want boots."

"No, you fool. It's not the boots or the horse or anything like that. It's the heart. Find what's in her heart. What her heart wants.

It's the finding that's the loving. Not the gift," Jack finished feeling like he had done pretty darn good for an old goat. He chuckled and his gaze went distant.

Blake shook his head. He knew both that sound and the look that went with it. Grandpa was thinking about Grandma. He was still in love with her. "I'll try, Grandpa."

\*

*He didn't exactly chuckle, but almost. His new disguise was going to work great on these small town hicks, he thought as he adjusted his bow tie. Especially here. He nodded as he twirled a single long stemmed red rose. The crisp Colorado air did nothing to refresh his mind, the beauty didn't touch him—only anger. Only blood.*

# CHAPTER 5

"Okay, that's enough for today," Kate yelled from her perch on the white pole fence. "Why don't you come on over?" She smiled at the three girls and two boys who made up her beginning horsemanship class as they each slowed their horses and walked to her.

Every other Saturday Kate taught three horsemanship classes. Out of the novice, intermediate, and advanced, this class was her favorite. Sure, she loved to see the flying lead changes and roll backs her other students could do with their mounts, but she loved this class the best. It was really special to see her students' hesitant movements become confident while their patient mounts went from confused tag-a-longs to willing partners.

"Miss White? My mom said you went parasailing out in California last weekend." Riley asked from atop his big roan. "What's parasailing anyway?"

"Was it fun?" asked Beth.

"Yeah, was it?"

"Was that city man nice?" asked Laura.

Kate looked at their smiling, expectant faces and smiled herself. "Yeah, he was nice and it was fun, kind of like flying. Not as fun as sitting up here on this cold fence grinding dirt with my teeth, but—"

The group giggled.

"Anyway, who can tell me what we learned today?" Kate asked them.

"We learned about lead changes," Kevin answered as he wiped his face with the back of shirtsleeve.

"What are they?" Kate grinned, knowing Kevin would get an ear full when he got home.

"We use gentle pressure with the reins and leg to guide our

horses in the direction we want them to go." Cathy looked up into the air visualizing the motions and repeating Kate's exact words.

"Great, now before you go. Keep your heels?"

"Down," the group replied.

Kate nodded. "Keep your face?"

"Up."

"And?"

"Keep a leg on each side and your mind in the middle," the group chorused with serious determination. They all felt honored to have such a phrase applied to their own lives. Rough stock competitors in the rodeo used the adage.

"Which means?" Kate asked and laughed as they each gave their own interpretation.

"Look where I'm going."

"Pay attention."

"Don't look at my hands."

"Keep my feet in the stirrups."

"Don't let go of the reins."

"You did great today. Go ahead and cool down your horses." Kate paused. She saw Luke out of the corner of her eye leaning against her truck, smiling. Waving at him, she went back to what she was saying. "No grain and no water yet. I'll be over in a minute to help." Kate made sure that each student made it out the gate and was on the way to the stables. "Hey, Luke, I didn't know you were coming," Kate said as she jumped down.

"I had to see you." Luke pulled her to him.

"I'm almost done. Been here long?"

"A little while. Did you enjoy the rodeo?" He kissed Kate's hand.

"Yeah. I won." She smiled.

Luke nodded. "I talked to Ranae. She said you'd be here. So I thought I'd come over and see if you were hungry."

"Starving. I haven't eaten since Green River, and that was just a muffin when I filled the tank."

"That's Utah, right?"

Kate laughed. "You wanna hang around? You can come meet the kids."

"I'm not exactly dressed for horse play." Luke flipped up the lapel on his suit jacket.

"No, I guess not." Kate laughed. Luke was always so clean-cut and neat. She liked having him as an addition to her life. She was tired of cowboys and their empty promises.

Well, one cowboy, anyway.

"Do what you need to. I'll be back in about forty-five minutes?"

"Sure. I'll get the kids on their way, then check on Lady Bug. You can at least meet her before we eat." Kate stood on her toes and kissed Luke's cheek. "I'll hurry."

\*

*Who the hell is that guy?* Blake wondered. He'd been watching his niece in Kate's horsemanship class and was standing near the watering trough. He'd have rather sat up on the fence beside Kate, but he figured he'd give her some space. He was pretty much forced to because she still wasn't returning his phone calls. He'd even tried to find her after the rodeo in Utah, but couldn't.

So he thought he might as well stay out of sight. That option was out of the question, now. He didn't like how that city guy was all duded up in his fancy suit and shiny shoes. He especially didn't like how he watched Kate walk away with that sly, smug damn-she's-cute-and-mine look on his face. Knock the front row of his teeth out, how 'bout that? Blake kicked at a clod of dirt and walked after Kate. The only person she ought to be kissing was him.

\*

Kate smiled for the first time in twenty or so hours. Luke was just what she needed to get over Blake. There we so many days he'd ruined. *No more! I'm going to enjoy the rest of my college days with Luke. We're going to…well, who knows, but we're going to do it,* she thought. *I can laugh with Luke. And dance. And eat. And I don't have to worry about Blake and his lies. Or his broken promises. Or his strong arms or his smooth voice. Or his—damn! I've got to quit this,* Kate chastised herself.

As patiently as she could manage, Kate got the kids to cool down their horses, water them and put them away. She had to repeat several times how to follow the horse's hair with the currycomb and to walk on the left side so the horse didn't get confused. She was pleased that she had to remind her students less and less to thank the horse for the hard work. She was as glad to see them wrapping their little arms around the horses' strong necks as she was to feel those same arms hold tight to her waist. With the final good-bye and promise to see them next Saturday, Kate looked at her watch. She had fifteen minutes before Luke would be back, and she still had a few more things to do.

Early springtime birds chirped their evening songs as Kate walked the distance to the practice pen. The ground beneath her feet was so familiar it felt as if it were her own. She had walked this path since she was nearly fifteen. She'd been so determined to get a job at Waldman Stables that she'd have ridden anything to prove her worth.

"I'll ride anything you have, Mr. Waldman," Kate's fifteen-year-old voice pleaded.

"There's no mister around here, kiddo. If you find one, you let me know. My name's Pete. Pete Waldman. And what d'ya mean—"

"I want to work here. I'm good with horses. I know how to work with them when they're lame. I know how to train them to lead, to saddle, to barrels. I'm learning how to rope, so I can do that pretty soon, too. Pete."

"What do you know about them?" Pete stretched his bulky six foot frame to its largest.

"I know I love 'em." Kate stretched her five-foot-four-frame to its tallest.

"Well, good to know. When can you start?"

Kate laughed at her memory as she folded her arms over the top rail of the pen. She owed Pete and Susan Waldman a lot. Not only did she have a job here to help pay for Lady's board, but she worked for Susan at the college in town. She wanted to make sure they never regretted all they had done for her. So she took extra care as she checked the latches on the practice pen gate and the round corral. She slowed her step as she walked the perimeter leading back to the stables. Her eyes scanned the ground for stray trash or wire, anything that might injure a horse.

Finding nothing, she paused a moment to massage the tired from her arms and stretch the muscles in her back and legs. She'd stayed in Utah just long enough to cool Lady down and hear if she'd won. Then she packed up and drove home. Blake was in the bareback event, and she didn't want to run into him again. She'd been up almost twenty-four hours. But she didn't complain, didn't even feel like it. The hours meant she was living the rodeo life. What were a few hours of sleep when she was living her dream, chasing cans and following the white lines on the highway?

She felt lucky, in fact that she was even still able to rodeo. She'd almost lost the chance when her mother had her first heart attack. Selling the ranch, the horses, and watching her mother's strong body age to a frail shadow of itself, was the hardest thing she'd ever done. Being able to keep Lady at Waldman Stables and continue to rodeo was a blessing that Kate wasn't about to forget.

The white-capped mountain peaks turned red in the fading light. The Sangre de Cristo range or the blood of Christ showed its namesake this night. Waldman Stables set out of town enough so that Kate could see all the mountains that surrounded the high valley. Their purple shades gave her peace as she wound her way between the watering trough and practice pen back to Lady's stall. A small breeze floated across the Rio Grande river. It brought with it the scent of newly blooming prairie flowers and young shoots of grass that grew at the edge of the river. The bright white pole fences linking the sables to the tall indoor arena grayed in the dusty twilight. Just outside Lady's stall a yellow light bulb shone a golden welcome to Kate, as did the candid smile of the cowboy who stood beneath it.

"Hello, Kate."

The fading light, the purple mountains and Blake's voice held Kate captive. The last time they'd been together below a sky with the moon just rising, had been after a rodeo years ago and they'd been dancing. They'd held onto each other as if the stars were their candles and the moon their wine. The only music playing was a waltz their hearts swayed to. The other dancer on their midnight dance floor was the summer breeze. It winked at them and teased them into kissing. Laughing and snuggling into their sleeping bag, the kiss grew. Kate could still feel Blake's lips on hers and his body warm above her. Her heart cried a little. The birds sang their last song as they roosted for the night. The world beyond the circle of light grew black and damp. Kate never felt so lonely.

"Guess you're probably wondering what I'm doing here?"

"It's late, Blake. I'm tired."

"Not too tired to be kissing that city feller." Blake could've kicked himself. He wanted to talk to her, not fight.

"That's none of your business. You have no right to be spying on me."

"I wasn't spying. I was watching Cathy."

Kate stepped into the full light. "Well, you should have taken her home and been on your way!"

Seeing dark circles beneath Kate's eyes, Blake studied her. He saw sadness and fatigue. "Jesus, Kate. Did you drive home last night? Have you even been home?"

"What do you care?"

Blake grabbed her arms. "Are you trying to kill yourself?"

"No. I'm living my life."

"I'll tell you what you're doing. You're going home and going to bed."

"Don't use that range boss voice on me. You have no right."

Blake couldn't listen to another word. Holding her body, even in anger, was too much for him. Her words were crushed against her mouth as his lips covered hers. He lifted her off her feet, molding her body to his. She'd been nineteen the last time he kissed her. Her body had grown and filled out since then. But he wasn't thinking of that. He wasn't thinking of anything, but how damn good it felt to just hold her, kiss her. Begging for her surrender, he stroked his hands over her hips, up her back, and fisted them in her hair.

The instant Kate felt Blake's mouth on hers, she froze. She was shocked at him. She was shocked at the wild flood of desire she felt. She knew she couldn't do this. But for a moment she let her body sink against his. It had been so long since she'd been touched, like this, by him. She wanted his hands on her, his body hard against hers, his lips demanding—just for a moment. She wound her arms around his neck and buried herself in him.

"Kate. Damn, Kate. I'm sorry." Blake set Kate down and stepped away.

Shame filled the space where desire had been. "Now, you're sorry again. Why don't you get it right, Blake! You're selfish. You only want what you want, when you want it."

"Hey, I wasn't the only one wanting here." Blake stepped forward.

Kate could feel his breath on her face. "Don't, Blake. Just get out of here."

"I didn't mean for this to happen. I just wanted to talk to you, spend some time with you."

"I think we've spent enough time together. You should go." Spinning away from him, Kate walked into Lady's stall, not waiting to see if Blake left. She took a few deep breaths and wiped her face, begging the tears not to come. "Hey, Lady Bug," she whispered as she flicked the switch to light Lady's stall. "What are you doing, lying down on the job?" Kate's voiced teased as she looked at her horse snuggled into the straw covering the floor.

Something didn't feel right. The usually warm stall felt odd, empty. Kate's eyes flew to Lady's side and watched for the smooth rhythm of her breathing. She saw none. "Lady?" She knelt at the horse's face. Felt for breath from her nose. There was none. "Lady Bug!" Kate sobbed a scream. "No! *No!*"

*

*The wind never stops blowing here, he thought as he looked into his mirror. He wiped his hand across his face, pulled it away covered in dirt and sweat. The filth on his fingers disgusted him. Shoving his hands under the faucet, feeling the warmth of the running water, he could easily imagine a different wet, a different heat. It won't be long now and it won't be dust I'll be washing down the drain, he thought with satisfaction.*

*He found the blood every time.*

# CHAPTER 6

"You're going out again." Ranae's voice filtered through the door and into the bathroom where Kate was getting ready. "Aren't you sick of him yet?"

"There's nothing else to do around here," Kate replied.

"Yes, there is. I thought we were going to go for ice cream in Cheyenne and that was weeks ago."

"Well, a lot's happened since then." Kate walked into the hallway where Ranae was.

"I know, but I think we should at least—"

"Should what Nae? I don't know what I'm doing. When I look at my future I don't see anything that I planned coming true. I get to graduate in May with my teaching degree, but now that Lady Bug is gone…beyond that I have no clue."

"I wish you wouldn't be so sad."

"I'm not sad. That's not the word."

"Well, mad then. But not everybody's life turns out like they plan, you know." Ranae crossed her arms and backed up.

"Damn it. I know that," Kate said as she wrapped her arms around Ranae. "I'm sorry for yelling."

"That's okay. I'm getting tougher. I don't let things people say, get to me, all the time."

"I know you are. But I just don't know what to do now that I'm almost finished with school. Get a teaching job, sure, but where? I don't want to quit riding to sit in one place nine or ten months out of twelve, teaching other people's kids so they get to where I am right now. With *nothing* as their future!"

"I know you're miserable. But maybe you could still find a way to rodeo. Don't people loan horses sometimes?"

"I won't do it without her." Kate swore when her chin trembled. "We were a team. She's all I had left."

"Well, we're your family now," Erin said as she walked up and wrapped her arms around them.

"We love you just as much as your mom and Lady Bug or even Blake ever could." Ranae squeezed both girls a little tighter and then stepped back saying, "And we had better get you ready for your date, even though I really don't want you to go."

"You're right. She is getting tougher." Erin smiled. Ranae's childhood had been horrible and abusive. It had been years since she'd had a single bruise, but confrontations were still hard. "Besides, Kate has to go. I have that web-cam thing hooked up to transmit part of their date to Nichole."

"I know," Ranae scolded, "but for two weekends in a row, you haven't even been in the state. Your first date to California worried me enough, but the weekend before last you went hot air ballooning in Lake Geneva, wherever that is, and then last weekend you went to New Orleans to visit dead people you don't even know."

"Lake Geneva is in Wisconsin and we did more than visit dead people in New Orleans, we went to practically every shop in The French Quarter, there was this amazing little trinket shop on Bourbon Street where I bought you that necklace and we ate Cajun catfish and listened to jazz."

"Awesome! When will the pictures be developed?" Erin asked, long ago coming to terms with Kate insisting that her pictures be developed and not just downloaded to a computer.

"We can pick them up tomorrow."

"How do you know you'll be here tomorrow?"

"Luke said we'd have a local date."

"What does that mean? You going to Texas, that's pretty close?" Ranae tapped her nails on the bathroom counter.

"No. We're staying here in town." Kate paused. "Nae, what's the matter?" Kate looked at her, surprised to find fear in her eyes instead of the teasing she was expecting. "What is it?"

"I don't know. I just can't put my finger on it, but I get more nervous for you every time you go anywhere with him." Ranae tried to smile and mask her fear. "Maybe I just miss you."

"I miss you guys, too," Kate said. "How about we do something tomorrow, all of us?"

"Oh yeah, we can go to the Pig," Ranae said. "It's a Saturday night after all."

"I hate that bar," Erin protested.

"You had fun the last time we were there," Ranae reminded her.

"Well, if we go it's going to be somebody else's turn to be the DD." Erin pointed at herself. "I have to be drunk to like that place. So I'm gonna to get piss-faced."

"It's my turn anyway," said Kate. "I'll be happy—" Kate stopped when the phone rang. "I'll get it. It might be Luke." Kate raced to the phone. "Hello, this is Kate."

"Well, you sound like you're doing fine, darlin'."

"What do you want, Blake?"

"Guess I wasn't who you were hoping to talk to."

"No, sorry, I was just expecting Nichole to call."

"Mmm-hmm."

"What do you want?"

"I was just callin' to say that we have some calves that were born late. Grandma and Grandpa, well all of us were goin' to hold a special branding for them." Blake paused. "It's tomorrow about noon. If you want to come."

"I kind of have plans with the girls."

"Oh. Well, that's okay." Blake's voice fell. "Maybe next time."

The phone clicked off before Kate could respond. She felt a moment of regret. She loved branding at the Spencers'. Leona was always such a blast, kicking around in her red boots, swearing at the cows and the cowboys like they didn't have any sense. Kate could hear her now, "You know I think if brains were feathers and you boys got together, you couldn't hardly make a pillow. Now you get over there and catch that calf. "

"What the hell did Blake want?" Erin interrupted her thoughts.

"He wanted me to go out to the branding they are having tomorrow."

"So late?" Erin might be the business major and look beautiful in a backless dress, but she could still muck around in a cow pasture and look like an ace doing it. Her father's daughter to the bone, she knew ranching.

"Just some that were born late," Kate said as the phone rang again. "Kate here," she answered.

"Hey. It's me." Nichole's voice sounded through the telephone. "I was just calling to say that I wish I could've stayed longer, but my boss wouldn't budge. He had a hard enough time understanding why I had to have leave in the first place."

"It's fine. *I'm* fine." Kate said, hoping that one day it would be true.

"Did the vet say anything different?"

"No. It's still pretty much the same."

"Do the cops have any leads?"

"No. I'm sure they have better things to do than find out who over-medicated my horse."

"I know we talked about this, but I just read in the paper about a girl who wanted to play varsity basketball and she had the top player injured so she could take her place. Do you think…?"

"Absolutely not. That doesn't happen in rodeo. We may be competing against each other, but—it just doesn't happen."

"Okay," Nichole said letting the topic drop. "What are you doing tonight? Are you and the girls going out or something?"

"Luke and I have plans."

"Good. I'm sorry I didn't get see him again while I was out there. It sounds like you guys have been having a lot of fun, Lake Geneva and New Orleans and all that. Have Erin hook up the webcam tonight so I can see you guys."

"Okay." Kate paused. "Hey, Nic?"

"Yeah."

"I didn't say it before, but thanks for being here."

"What are best friends for?"

Kate knew Nichole would be smiling as she hung up. The best friends statement was something left over from high school when the world's biggest problems could be solved with an ice cream cone and movie rental. But somewhere between the mint chocolate chip and Gerard Butler, Kate's life had fallen apart.

"What'd Nichole want?" Ranae asked.

"She just wanted to make sure Erin was going to set up the webcam so she could see Luke and me tonight."

"Good God! She's hounded the hell out of me about that! We are doing it today! I don't want any more of her yapping—" Erin's voice changed into an impression of Nichole's. "'I want to see Luke and Kate together.' Flap-flap-flap. I'm sick of it. So if we aren't expecting more phone calls, let's get logged onto the internet." Erin pressed the power button on her laptop. "She's going to start complaining now about how you guys don't have wireless! Yap! Dial-up is slow. Yap! *Yap!*"

"No, we aren't expecting any more calls. I just want to finish getting ready."

Kate walked back to the bathroom. As she twisted the wand of the mascara and brushed it through her lashes, she began to feel anxious about the evening. She didn't want the girls to know, because she hoped it was just a phase, but the constant attention Luke gave and expected was a bit overwhelming. When they were walking along Jackson Square in New Orleans, Kate had wanted to put her hair up because of the heat. She'd released Luke's hand to reach in her purse for a hair band.

Luke instantly questioned, "What are you doing?"

"I'm putting up my hair. I'm hot."

"Don't you want to hold my hand?"

"Of course I do. I just need two hands to do this." Kate smiled and when finished, she immediately reached for his hand and gave it a squeeze, thinking that he must have had a rough time growing up. He seemed really insecure. She'd tried that night to ask him about his parents.

He responded with, "Why, don't you think I'm good enough? Do you have to meet them to prove it?"

Kate tried to apologize, and say of course he was good enough and that she was only making conversation, but it took him several hours to get back to his normal cheery mood. *I'll have to be more patient*, Kate thought as she finished applying the gloss to her lips.

Without wanting him to, Blake came to mind. What to do about him? With him came ranching and cows and rodeos, everything she wanted. Then what am I doing with Luke? Kate shook her head. She knew the answer. Luke was easier. Her heart wasn't involved. There was too much pain when it came to Blake. He represented everything she couldn't have. And she couldn't trust him.

The doorbell rang.

"Luke's here." Ranae walked to the door.

Hearing Nae open the door and greet Luke, meant her time was up, when it came to solving problem number two. Looking in the mirror, Kate took several deep breaths. The girl that stared back wasn't anyone Kate knew. She looked as hollow and exhausted as Kate felt. She'd felt this way since she'd stood in the rain smelling of diesel fumes and hearing the low rumble of the backhoe as it filled Lady's grave with dirt. Smoothing her palms down Erin's black Levis and peach shirt, Kate slipped on a pair of Ranae's brown loafers. The rodeo clothes were gone, just as the rodeo was.

"Well, I have this thing all ready to go," Erin said when Kate walked out of the bathroom. "I've explained it to your dude here and he knows what to do."

Luke stood and pulled Kate in front of the monitor's camera, swept her in a long dip, kissed her cheek and pulled a red rose from behind his back. "For you," he smiled.

"Thank you." Kate stood, smelled the rose and talked to Nichole through the camera. "This is Luke. You remember him, I'm sure. He and I are off to eat and watch a movie. I love you, bye." Kate waved.

Erin waved to Nicole through the screen. "Happy now? Sheesh!" Then she shut the lid to her laptop.

"Well, I guess we'll go," Kate said to Erin and Ranae and walked toward the door.

"Kate," Ranae interrupted, "just a second." She glanced toward Luke.

"Luke, why don't you go on out, and I'll meet you in a few minutes." Kate smiled and squeezed Luke's hand.

Luke nodded and shut the door behind him.

"What is it, Nae?"

"I don't know. I don't think you should go. I can't seem to shake the feeling that you're in danger." Ranae shook her head. "You know how you said you fell asleep on the way to California? I didn't want to bring this up before, but what if you were drugged or something?" Fear accented every word.

"Nae, that only happens in big cities. And I was really sleepy. You know I'd been out the night before trying to photograph the moon. The car ride just made me groggy, and I never drink champagne. I had two glasses."

"It doesn't just happen in big cities," called Erin from the computer. "I have a cousin who lives in Durango and it happened to her. But I think she'd been doing other drugs, though. Hell, I don't know how that drug works. I don't even know what in the hell it's called. He'd better hope to hell he didn't try any shit. We'll kick his ass to hell and back!" Every word got louder.

"Enough with the hells already," Ranae said as she took hold of Kate's arm. Real fear showed on her face. "The airport is only five miles away. How could you fall asleep in five miles?"

"Oh, you guys, what's he going to do here in town? If he was going to do anything, don't you think he would have done it by now?"

"Maybe," Ranae said.

"I think I should go. He's waiting for me."

"Well, at least come home early," Ranae said. "I'll wait up."

"Shit, I guess I will, too." Erin turned off her computer. She unhooked everything and was plugging the cord back into the phone as Kate shut the door.

Immediately, the phone rang.

Erin picked it up. "Hello."

"Erin, Oh my god." Nichole's voice cried. "Has Kate left? Don't let her!"

"Shit, Ranae, go get Kate," Erin yelled.

Ranae bolted out the door. She could hear Nichole's voice crying, *"Don't let her go!"*

"Nichole," Erin said into the phone, "Nichole. Nichole! What the hell's going on?

"She's gone." Ranae came running back.

"Oh, no! Call the police. He has to be stopped." Erin clicked on the speaker so Ranae could hear Nichole. "I knew it that night in The Pub. I knew I recognized him, but I couldn't place him. And I didn't say anything because I was glad Kate had found someone besides Blake. I forgot about my suspicion. Damn it!"

"Nichole, just tell us who he is," sobbed Ranae.

"He's the Red Rose Serial Killer," Nichole's hoarse voice whispered.

"What the hell are you talking about?" Erin yelled.

"Don't you guys watch television? He's all over the news. He always gives the girl a red rose on the night he's going to rape and kill her," Nichole raged. "This guy's a murderer. Call the police." The phone went dead. Nichole sobbed and prayed for Kate as she dialed the number of her travel agent. She was going home.

*

As soon as Nichole started yelling to call the police, Ranae grabbed her cell phone from her purse. "Oh God!" Her fingers shook as she struggled to turn it on and dial 911. While she ranted at the police to go find this guy, Erin called the only other law in town, the Spencer's.

She swore as it rang and yelled into the receiver as soon as Leona picked it up, "I need to speak to Blake Spencer right damn now. It's about Kate!"

Since Erin had called to cuss at him a time or two in the past when he had made Kate cry, Blake didn't know whether to come to the phone or not. Something in his gut told him to. When he heard what was going on, he grabbed his rifle and headed to the door. Jack and Leona weren't far behind him in their truck.

*

*He'd tried to keep the anger away, but it was his master. It won. He needed to do what it commanded. "Kill her," the beast said. "Kill them all."*

# CHAPTER 7

As Kate walked with Luke through the door of The Out West Steakhouse and into the dimly lit air-cooled seating area, she tried to push her friends' worries out of her mind. In their place came other thoughts.

The last time she'd come here was with Blake. They'd sat in the corner by the potted tree at that round table with the flickering candle. They'd had crab legs. It was her birthday and they'd ridden horses all day. She'd worn the red dress she and Nichole had just purchased.

Absentmindedly, Kate sat in the chair the waiter pulled out for her.

"Hello. Where are you?" Luke tapped his fingers on the table. "You've been being weird all night."

"I'm sorry, Luke. I'm just having a bad day, I guess. This place is really nice. The chicken fried steak is good."

Luke nodded to the waitress. Both of them would have the same. "I'm sorry you're having a bad day. Do you want to talk about it?"

"Not really. It's the same as it's been. I just miss Lady Bug." And Blake.

"Okay." Luke shrugged his shoulders. "What movie do you want to see tonight? There is a new one that seems funny. I think that—"

As Luke talked, Kate looked around and remembered one of the best nights of her life. Blake had been so handsome and so nervous that night. It had been their first real date. Kate remembered how he had peeled her crab legs for her because he didn't want the shell to be rough on her hands. I need you, Blake, Kate almost whispered.

"Kate, your food is here."

"Oh." Kate noticed for the first time that there was indeed food in front of her. "I didn't mean to spoil the evening. It's just that this place has some memories that aren't easy for me."

"What kind of memories?"

"Old rodeo stuff."

"Maybe we'll take another trip."

"I think that's easier on me than being here in town."

"Well, eat your food."

Kate ate as much of her food as she could then went to the restroom. Taking a few deep breaths and pressing her hand to her churning stomach, she tried to clear her mind. Luke was being strange, the same as he'd been in New Orleans. *But so am I*, she reminded herself. *No wonder he's upset. I was so preoccupied that I didn't even notice my food was right in front of me.* Vowing to do better, Kate went to meet him. He was pacing and Kate smiled as brightly as she could.

"I'm ready." Kate looked at her shoes and wondered how she could feel so lost in her own body. She wasn't used to the roller coaster of emotions she felt when she was with Luke.

"Fine."

"Thank you for the great meal. The chicken fried steak was good, wasn't it?" Kate tried to lighten the mood. It seemed to work too, because by the time they were back at her place, he was chattering away about some crazy thing he had seen on TV.

"It's barely eight. Do you mind if I come in?" Luke smiled. "Maybe we could find something to watch." He reached behind the seat and brought out another red rose and held it out for Kate to take.

"Thanks." Kate took the rose. "I think that staying here is fine. And speaking of staying here, I wanted to talk to you about next weekend," she continued as they walked into the apartment. She had a brief moment of surprise when she saw that it was empty. "The girls and I haven't been able to do much lately and they're feeling a little neglected. So we wanted to spend tomorrow together, if that's okay?" Kate shut the door to the apartment behind them and locked it out of habit.

"It's a guy you remember, isn't it?" Luke's voice was crude and completely different from the calm voice Kate had always known. He ripped the rose she carried from her hand.

"What do you mean?"

"I'm going to give you something to remember," Luke whispered into her ear as he spun her to face him and slammed her back against the wall with his weight. He ground his mouth against Kate's. His grip bruised her shoulder. Holding her in place, he ripped his mouth away.

"No. No. I don't know what you mean."

Kate tried to talk. A fast sharp slap shocked her silent. Then his mouth was back, harder and more vicious. Kate tasted blood. Her stomach clenching tight, she tried to escape his iron hold. Grabbing and bending his fingers back, she tried to move. Edging to the door, she tried the knob. Locked. His laugh filled the air.

"You'll never forget me."

His breath seemed to rot the air. He slid the long stemmed red rose around her throat. The thorns tore her flesh. Kate fought him.

He laughed. He pushed her.

She slammed to the carpet. Dimness filled the air. Time seemed to stand still. Her breathing raced. *Get away*, screamed through every part of her. Kicking. Biting. Crying. She caught hold of his skin and scraped with her nails. Her fingers felt sticky.

"Bitch!" Luke screamed, feeling warm blood on his face.

"Why are you doing this?"

"You deserve it." Luke laughed. "It's extravagant, don't you think? I've never given you a rose before. I think it's time." Luke yanked Kate up to face him. He slapped her face with the rose he held. The thorns cut deep. Luke took her hand and twirled her into a dip. Crushing the rose, he let the petals fall above her. They drifted like drops of blood to touch her face. His grip imprisoned her, but his lips grew soft.

They moved their way to Kate's mouth, when they were barely touching her lips Luke said, "I've waited long enough."

He jerked her to her feet and released her. His eyes held hers. Those same eyes that always seemed so searching were indeed searching, for weakness. Using the evil they possessed to crush her like he did the rose.

Fear sank in Kate's gut. But courage was there, too. She used the moment of freedom to run.

Luke grabbed her from behind and flung her to the floor. His body smashed into hers. "Shall I put your hair up for you?" His voice grated as he grabbed it by the handfuls and jerked it up. Where hairline met neck, his lips burned as he ground his teeth. Kate stopped trying to push up from the floor and started feeling around for something.

"What are you doing?" Luke captured her shoulders and twisted her to face him.

She couldn't get up. His legs were clamped around her back. Looking at him through the dim light she could see his face framed in fury. She saw the shiny glint of a blade. Panic grew from deep inside. The screaming turned to a roar pounding inside her head. Squeezing her eyes shut, Kate held her breath waiting.

Luke pressed the cold steel to her neck.

*Live! Fight! Live!* The words chanted, roared, echoed through her brain. Kate tried to push away from the knife. The blade seared her flesh. She kept fighting. She kept living. Eyes open and filled with panic, she struggled. She didn't notice the deep gash in her arm or the rushing blood. She fought. Kicked, screamed, crawled.

He ripped her shirt away.

The air felt frigid.

"No!" Kate lunged up and pushed him back. His fist spun and connected.

"No." She curled into a ball, sobbing. Holding her throbbing face. Keep your eyes open. *Live! Fight!* Her eyes stung with tears.

Kicking her legs, she tried to reach him, but he caught them, first one and then the other. Kate felt the cold sharp steal of the knife as it cut in a slow rhythm. The knife traveled the seams of her pants from her ankles all the way to her waist. She could hear the ripping. She was beyond fear now. *Please someone help me*, she prayed. Trembling and crying, she tried to crawl away.

"You will remember me. I promise." Luke laughed. "When you dream, in that time just before death, you will dream of me. I will be the last face you see, just as I was the last face your precious, horse saw."

He laughed as she screamed. He ripped her hair. Her head snapped back. Her body whipped flat before him. Meticulous and slow, he put the sharp edge to her throat. Kate could feel his dirty gaze eat at her naked skin. He scraped his body over hers, his slimy, hot tongue licking as he went.

"You bastard!" Kate screamed. Her frantic, searching hand grasped a hard cool object. Taking hold, thinking clear. One chance. Once just once. Slam. She smashed it into Luke's head. He didn't move. She pushed at his rancid form. She was on her knees. She was on her feet. She ran to the door. He was on her again.

"You god damn whore. You'll pay for that," Luke screamed. His fists pounded Kate's body.

Blackness was coming. Haze clouded her vision. From a distance she could hear Luke scream, "Are you dreaming? Kate, are you? Look at me, you whore."

She could see the edge of the dark, but she kept fighting. Screaming! Striking! Hitting! Clawing! Hitting—nothing. Was he gone? She tried to see. Tried to blink. Too many tears. Too much blood. Too much pain. Dimly she heard a crash and felt a light.

She couldn't see. She could feel herself drifting to the edge. Beyond it would be freedom. Maybe Lady Bug would be in heaven. Maybe there would be a rodeo. But someone was talking. Who? Mama? A man.

"Oh, Jesus. Kate, darlin'," sobbed the man's voice as he reached to touch her.

Kate looked. She tried to see through the blood stinging her eyes. "No! Get away!" She scrambled away.

"Darlin'. It's me. It's Blake. You're safe now." He tried desperately to keep his voice soft and calm.

"Blake? You're here." Kate sobbed. Gentle arms wrapped a blanket around her shaking body.

*

Blake looked at Kate. Her long, beautiful hair was matted with her blood. Her green eyes streamed with tears of fear. Smears of blood covered her face, her body. Bruising fist marks were beginning to show beneath her skin. Deep gashes cut her hands and arms.

Fury like he had never known sliced his heart. He had a rifle in his truck. He saw the guy. He knew every inch of his stinking hide. Burning hate for him ignited when Blake heard Kate's screams through the door. It broke like kindling. Blake saw him, the sniveling coward. He ran. He couldn't have run too far. *I am fast and sure. I can make him pay.* But he would not have left the sobbing body in his arms for any amount of revenge. So instead of moving away from her, he pulled her closer. He felt her tense. The anger surged again, but still he stayed.

"Ranae," Blake called.

"Yes." Ranae's panicked voice answered.

"We should call the police, again."

"I already did. I told them what happened and they said not

to do anything, but just wait for them. What am I going to do? I'm so sorry, Kate. This is all my fault," Ranae huddled with Erin sobbing.

"No, it isn't. If you hadn't called—all of you could have been hurt. I just hope we got here in time. Before—before he—" Blake couldn't finish. It was too horrible to even think much less say. All he felt was rage, plain and simple. Rage in its purest form.

Ranae just cried over and over. "I hope so too. Please God I hope so. I hope he didn't rape her." Ranae's cries echoed through the apartment.

# CHAPTER 8

A terrified Ranae opened the apartment door at the police chief's knock on the door. As she did so, Erin walked out saying, "Nae, I'm not leaving. I'm right here, but I can't take this shit any longer. I'm gonna try Nichole again. Maybe she'll answer this time."

Crying and nodding, Ranae clung to the door as if it were the only thing holding her up. Wringing her hands, she let in the police chief. He had to duck to come through the doorway. The deep blue of his uniform matched the concern in his eyes.

"I'm Ranae. Kate's roommate." She held out her shaky hand.

"Chief of Police, Aaron Barrs." He reached for her hand, holding onto it for a moment before releasing Ranae to rake a hand through his graying black hair. As though preparing himself for the worst, he stepped into the room where Blake sat with Kate on the couch.

Barely contained fury evident in every movement, Blake stood and motioned toward Kate. "I'm Blake Spencer and this is Katherine White."

Drawing in a deep breath, Barrs came forward. "Katherine, my name is Aaron Barrs. I'm the Chief of Police. I'd like to talk with you if you're up to it."

"People call me Kate." Kate looked at the crisscrossing patterns on the blanket that covered her.

"I need to take some pictures and ask you about what happened. Then we'll go to the hospital. We have an ambulance waiting." He gave her a quick appraisal, taking note of the towel wrapping her right arm. "I'm going to ask a female officer and one of the paramedics to come in. The officer is for your comfort while the paramedic examines you and bandages your arm while we talk." He unlatched the radio from his shoulder and spoke into it.

When the officer and the paramedic had joined them, Barrs said, "We'll need to photograph your injuries and the scene. I'll also need you to tell me exactly what happened."

Glancing up for the first time, Kate nodded. "If we take the pictures first, can we start cleaning?"

Barrs stared at her blood-smeared face. The cut on her chin had stopped bleeding; the area around her left eye showed the start of a huge fist-shaped bruise. "It might be a while before you can start cleaning," he said gently. "Our forensics team will need to gather as much evidence as possible."

Kate shivered. "We can't leave this mess."

"Sure we can," Ranae said through the tears streaming down her cheeks. "We can do anything we want."

"Right." Barrs turned to nod at the female officer. "Make sure you document all of her injuries and get pictures of her face." He looked back at Kate. "You just rest with your friends here and we'll be done as quickly as we can."

While Barrs and his officer moved around the room, Blake sat beside Kate, afraid to touch her for fear of hurting her more. He desperately wanted to hold her, to absorb the pain she was experiencing, to go back to the time before anything had happened to her. Most of all he wanted to bash in the guy's head who'd done this to her. Instead all he could do was watch the paramedic.

When the paramedic unwrapped the towel from her arm, Kate hissed in a painful breath. Unable to watch any longer, Ranae turned and fled, sobbing, to the kitchen, the misery of her abusive childhood sharp in her mind. Barrs entered the kitchen behind her.

"Ranae?" He stood beside the sink and watched her turn on the tap, fill a glass. "May I ask you a few questions?"

"I guess." Ranae turned off the water.

"We've been in touch with you throughout the evening. I have that all down, but what I need is for you to tell me what you saw when you came home."

Ranae put down the glass of water and clutched the edge of the sink without looking at the chief. "The first thing is what I heard. I heard Kate screaming. We rushed in as fast as we could. Blake broke the door. It was dark in here so I turned on the lights. Kate was on the living room floor. This guy Luke was beat—" Ranae sobbed. She tried to catch her breath. She squeezed her eyes shut.

"It's okay. Take your time."

"Beating her. It's like he was crazy. We surprised him. He ran past us. We didn't try to go after him because of Kate. She was naked and bleeding and screaming." Her hands trembled and she tightened her grip on the sink. "It was awful. Blake got a blanket and covered her. He tried to comfort her while I called you again."

"Luke, you said his name was? Was he fully dressed?" Aaron asked.

"Yes, I think so. I'm not sure. I didn't really look at him. I just wanted Kate to be okay."

"Do you know Luke's last name?"

"Ferral. Luke Ferral. He just started college here. We never really met him until a couple of weeks ago down at the The Pub."

"Thanks, Ranae." Barrs looked at his notes. "That's all for now. Let's go talk to Kate."

They returned to the living room where the paramedic had finished with Kate's arm and started to clean her face. Anything more would have to wait until the rape team finished with her at the hospital.

Blake paced. He hated the sense of helplessness that came with not knowing how to make things better instantly.

"Mr. Spencer, as soon as I am finished asking Kate some questions, I'll have some for you as well," Barrs told him.

Blake nodded. "No problem, I'll be right here. Or anywhere Kate goes. So I'll be easy to find."

Barrs turned to Kate. "Kate," he said kindly, "can you tell me what happened?"

"Luke and I went to dinner. At the Out West Steakhouse near the rodeo grounds. The one where Blake and I went to years ago and had crab legs."

The statement gave Blake a glimmer of hope.

"Luke got mad…" Kate continued in some confusion. "I fell asleep…We flew to California…." She shook her head.

Barrs looked at Ranae in confusion.

"She's talking about a few weekends ago. I don't think Luke was mad at her then. It was their first date."

"I didn't stop fighting," Kate breathed. "Mama, I was strong."

The confusion and jumbled words split Blake's heart. *"Dolly, be strong,"* were the last words Kate's mom had said before she left for Oregon. The memory might have just saved Kate's life. Blake reached for her hand.

She flinched.

"Sorry, Kate." The whisper was so soft Kate didn't hear him.

"He was going to kill me. He killed Lady Bug." Kate rocked back and forth as tears spilled down her cheeks.

"Take your time," Barrs soothed.

Kate tried to begin again. "I'm alive." She stopped again and bent her head. "I didn't give up. I hit him with it." Kate pointed to a huge gray rock that she and Erin had found at the river. "I ran. He caught me. I kept fighting." Her lips trembled and tears fell in torrents. "I didn't give up." She looked up at Blake. "I didn't give up." She saw tears in his eyes as well. And, anger so intense it was frightening. She looked away.

"Kate, I have to ask you one more question," Barrs said quietly. Kate looked to him. "Did Luke rape you?"

Shame filled Kate. How she could have been so stupid as to trust Luke… Pain and anger threatened her emotions, but she went on with determination. "No. I didn't let him. I fought him."

She looked at Blake. Relief washed his face, but the rage in his eyes remained.

"Okay, that's good," Barrs told her. He gestured at the paramedics. "I think we're ready to send you to the hospital."

When Ranae and Erin had bundled Kate up and helped her out the door with the paramedics following them, Barrs turned to Blake.

"Do you need to question me?" asked Blake.

"Yes, I just need to know what you saw when you came in the door."

"Red," Blake said.

"Yes, I can imagine." Watching Blake carefully, the police chief tapped his sidearm. "If that were to happen to my daughter, I wouldn't think twice about using my pistol."

Blake's jaw worked. "Well, I have to be honest. The thought crossed my mind when I saw what the bastard had done. Then, when I held her and she let me, I knew there wasn't anything that was going to drag me away."

"Good to know, son. We don't need any vigilante justice here."

"Too bad," Blake responded. "As to what I saw, when I came in…"

*

The emergency room was a feverish place filled with accident victims, stoic faces, and illness. A quiet, blonde nurse met Kate and her friends when the ambulance came in, whisked them immediately into a private exam room and punched a button on the wall to call a doctor. She arrived within moments.

"Hello, Kate. I'm Stephanie Thorns, but you can call me Stevie." She smiled at Kate who sat on the examining table. "I specialize in cases like yours."

Kate hunched into her shoulders. "Hi," she said.

"Who are your friends here?" Stevie pointed to Ranae, Erin and Blake sitting on the hard yellow chairs nearby.

"This is Ranae, my roommate, and Erin. And this is…" Kate paused. "Blake."

"Pleased to meet you. You guys are welcome to be here for the first part of the exam, but pretty soon I'll ask you to wait in the other room." She smiled when they exchanged terrified looks. "I know it's silly to tell you not to worry, that I'll take good care of Kate, that she's safe here, but I'll say it anyway. Kate will have the best possible care, but you have to let me give it to her. It means I'll have to make a full examination both in order to make certain she's all right and to collect as much evidence as possible so that the police can catch the man who did this to her." She turned to Kate. "Kate, if you'd like your roommate to stay with you, we can do whatever will make you most comfortable. My examination will be thorough, though, and I know you'll want as much privacy as possible for that."

Trembling, Kate exchanged glances with each of her friends in turn, then nodded at the doctor. "Nae, can you…?" she whispered.

Ranae's hands twisted in her lap and her eyes moved fearfully taking in the sterile exam room, but she dipped her head once in assent.

Ranae's clearly telegraphed "been here" terror was not lost on the doctor, but all she only smiled a quick thank you and said, "Good," before glancing at the others.

"Nae, I'm going to get some coffee and try to call Nichole again," Erin said.

Blake nodded, not taking his eyes off Kate.

"Okay. I'm going to stay here." Ranae reached to hug Erin. "I love you."

"I—you," Erin paused. "Tell Kate." Erin turned and grabbed Blake's arm. "You can't stay here," she told him.

He shook his head.

Kate tried to look at him, but couldn't meet his eyes. "Please, Blake," she whispered, "don't make this harder. Just go."

"Kate, I—"

The doctor intervened. "Kate's going to need fresh clothes," she said in a kind voice. "It would help her a lot if someone would go get them."

Blake looked at Kate, who nodded. "Please," she whispered again. Blake went.

\*

On the way back to the apartment Blake was darkly silent, but still unable to reach Nichole, Erin chattered anxiously.

"I can't stand to think what might have happened to Kate if you and Jack and Leona hadn't come. Where are they anyway?"

"They went back to the ranch. The figured they'd see her tomorrow."

"I'm glad you came," Erin told him.

Irritation swept Blake. "Of course I came. Kate needed me. I should have been with her tonight. Not him." He hit the steering wheel with his hand.

"It's not your fault. You're not the one who told her to go have fun when Ranae had the feeling something was wrong and wanted her to stay home, I am. If it's anyone's fault it's mine, not yours."

She was still running on in the same vein when they reached the apartment. It wasn't until Blake grabbed her arm and pointed that she noticed the note and the deep red rose lying on the sidewalk in front of the door.

"Oh my God," she breathed.

Unease prickled through Blake. Even knowing that he shouldn't touch what might turn out to be evidence, he bent to retrieve the square of white and opened it. Scribbles of blue ink proclaimed tersely, *I am not through with you yet.*

Erin swallowed. "He didn't leave." She caught Blake's arm and spun around searching. "Why didn't the police find him?"

Fury coursed through Blake and came out in a curse. "He ran, the bastard, then came back. I'm sure he's gone now." Another oath bit the air as the thought completed itself. He spun back toward his truck. "Kate's not here, she's at the hospital. He would know that. Let's go." Reaching the truck, he felt behind the seat and pulled out his rifle.

Shocked, Erin stumbled when she saw the gun. "Why would he go there? There's too many people. There's the police. We don't have her clothes."

"He didn't care how many people saw him before he attacked her, did he?" Blake shouted as he slid behind the steering wheel. "Get in. We'll make do for her clothes."

Erin had barely shut the passenger-side door behind her when he gunned the truck's motor and tore out of the parking lot.

They arrived at the hospital to find Kate perfectly safe with Ranae, the bleary-eyed doctor, and the same female police officer who'd been with Chief Barrs earlier.

"She can go home," the doctor was telling both the officer and Ranae when Blake barged in. "I have my report and she said she doesn't want to stay the night. Since she didn't lose consciousness during the attack, she probably doesn't have a concussion, but if the gash on her head were any deeper, I'd make her. I've stitched up both her head and her arm as well." She turned to Kate. "Be gentle when you wash and keep the stitches dry." Back to Ranae. "She's got pain medication and I gave her something to help her sleep tonight." She glanced at Blake and looked at Erin who rushed in to stand behind him. "She'll be fine in body, if you guys stay with her." To Kate. "Emotionally it will take time."

She watched the girls fuss over Kate as they again wrapped in her blanket and helped her out. Then she looked hard at Blake. "A minute?"

"Yes?" Blake answered turning.

"It's easy to see that you care about Kate."

"Yes. I do."

"Just make sure that your anger toward the guy who did this to her doesn't show so much that she thinks it's directed at her. Be careful. She's very strong, but she'll need more love and patience to deal with this than anyone imagines right now."

Blake nodded. "Thanks, Doc. I'll do my best."

He walked out reflecting that the doctor had made sense. He wasn't sure if he could mask his feelings toward Luke entirely, but if it would help Kate, he'd sure as hell try.

*

When they returned to the apartment, Ranae helped the shivering and exhausted Kate pull her bed down for the night. Despite the doctor's orders to keep her stitches dry, Kate needed to take a shower before she went to sleep. She could still feel Luke's dirty hands and body on her and she needed to do whatever she could to erase that, scrub away the filth from the night's events.

Her mind refused to shut off.

Both Ranae and Erin insisted that someone should be with her at all times. Intellectually, Kate knew they were only trying to help, to make sure no one ever harmed her again, but she wanted space, needed relief from their panicked hovering. She tried to convince them that she could shower alone, but the duo wouldn't listen. In an effort at compromise, only Erin sat on the counter in the bathroom while Kate let the hot water wash over her until it ran cold.

Still she didn't feel clean.

Blake and Erin had discussed the note with Ranae; among the three of them, they decided not to tell Kate about it or the rose until they absolutely had to. They did, however, finally decide it would be prudent to inform Chief Barrs.

"No, he's gone. We can't find him." Barrs's muffled voice came through Blake's cell.

"What are you going to do?"

"Well, between what was collected on scene and what was collected from Kate herself at the hospital, we have all the evidence we can get—for now. The forensics team combed the place after you guys went to the hospital. We have to wait to see what comes of that. But between the description you all gave us and that video cam set up from before Kate went out, we have an excellent idea of who we're looking for. The best we can do unless something more comes up is keep looking. And I've arranged for a patrol car to keep tabs on the apartment for the next few days."

"No need," Blake assured him. "I'll be here."

The chief made a noncommittal noise that spoke volumes. "Nevertheless," he said. He let the one word hang for a moment before continuing. "Ideally, I'd like to move Kate to a secure location where we can monitor anyone who attempts to contact or approach her, but she also needs to be with her friends, people she trusts completely, right now."

"I'm not leaving her," Blake said. "No matter what it takes, she'll be safe."

"That's what I'm afraid of," Barrs responded baldly.

Blake ignored him. "Also, I want to know about anything you find." His voice held all the authority of generations of Spencers.

Barrs recognized the tone. He'd grown up with it, respected it. That didn't mean he liked the implications behind it. "I'll do what I can. But you have to know that anything that leaks out of this office—even if it's only to you—and jeopardizes our investigation jeopardizes Kate as well. Especially, if it means we can't keep the sonofabitch in jail once we catch him."

"If I have anything to say about it, he'll be in the ground before prison becomes an issue," Blake muttered to himself.

Barrs heard him, but only cleared his throat and said, "You can't help her if you're in prison yourself, Blake Spencer, so keep your head about you, son."

Blake's jaw clenched as he worked over the truth of that statement. "Will do," he agreed finally and disconnected.

He glanced around at the chaos Luke had created in the apartment. Every drop of blood ignited the fuse on his anger. Every broken item and fingernail scratch in the fabric of the couch infuriated him. The rose petals caked with blood stopped his breath.

He started to clean.

After his third trip to the kitchen to fill a bucket with clean, soapy water, he went out to his truck to swear and kick the dirt. Then he checked the area for anyone who might be lurking. Returning to the apartment, he again made sure his rifle was loaded. Nobody was hurting Kate again. Nobody! He would make sure of that.

\*

Kate knew when the girls finally forced her out of the shower and into some warm, comfort clothes, but she couldn't remember how or when she got into bed. She had a vague sense of having heard Blake, Erin, and Ranae whispering together over her head, followed by the sensation of being covered in blankets. She remembered praying that the pills given to her at the hospital would make it so she wouldn't dream.

She didn't.

Blake didn't either. His eyes never closed. The cool barrel of his rifle lying across his lap was the only comfort he felt that night.

# CHAPTER 9

The dull, gray building that housed the prosecutor's offices loomed in front of Kate. It was her second visit to them and Todd Vernon, the assistant prosecutor who was prepping her case. She glanced at the pair with her: Nichole, who had arrived the day after the attack, and Blake, who'd refused to leave her for any space of time since. She was grateful to them both for their presence, but her own constant need to be surrounded by people she knew was beginning to irk her. She hated the feeling of having lost control of her life because of the brutal actions of one man.

Tucking the ear buds attached to her MP3 player back into her ears, Kate flipped quickly through the songs she'd been listening to lately and pressed play. Escape from reality came with Dan Seals singing about the way a cowgirl rode out wearing rhinestones and sequins on a sunlit evening. There was comfort in the rodeo songs; they were taking her back to the way things had been when rodeo, her horse, and loving Blake was all she knew. It might not be the fastest way to move on from the attack, but dealing with the present wasn't easy either. So she lost herself in the music, and even standing right outside the prosecutor's office, let herself fade into the past.

Standing beside her, Blake's thoughts were black. No matter how hard he tried, he couldn't get the image of Kate's bloodied, beaten body out of his mind. Every time he saw her, his fury took on new dimensions. He wanted Luke and his evilness bloodied and ground to dust. He hated himself for not being where Kate had needed him. For thinking that striking out on his own in order to make a life to bring her into was the best thing to do. For always thinking that he had to be the one to find the ways and the means by himself, instead of being *there* any of the times she'd needed him. Because he couldn't be. Couldn't bear to see her in pain. This time would be different, though. He might not know what to do for her, but he knew that this time he would be there. Here. Wherever. He wasn't going anywhere.

"I'm going to get it right this time," he muttered.

Surprised, Nichole looked over. "Get what right?"

Blake winced. "Did I say that out loud?"

Nichole smiled. "You've said a lot of things out loud lately when you were sure Kate wasn't listening."

Blake sighed. "Fine. So if I tell you I never really knew what to do before when Kate was sad or crying, it won't come as a surprise."

Nichole swallowed a grin and shook her head. "Not so much. I take it this came as a lightning bolt for you, though?"

"Well…" Blake grimaced. "I've thought about it before. But just now I realized how much it hurt Kate that I couldn't or didn't deal with it. I was more concerned about how much her hurting, hurt me." He looked at Nichole. "Does that make sense?"

She nodded.

"I was an idiot." His lips twisted. "Not any more, though. Or at least," he amended, "not in the same way."

"Maybe we should go inside." Ready as possible to face the present, Kate pulled the buds from her ears and looked at them.

Smiling sadly, Blake nodded and tugged the huge wooden door before them open. It creaked on its hinges as they went through. Vernon's secretary looked up when they entered.

"Miss White," she said. "Mr. Vernon is expecting you. I'll tell him you're here." She stood and stiletto-clicked the short distance to his office. "He'll be with you shortly," she confirmed, when she came back.

Kate nodded. Suddenly nervous, she twisted her fingers together until Blake noticed and slipped one of his hands into hers. She flinched—then berated herself for the weakness. He wasn't her molester and he was there to help. She swallowed and tried to smile at him.

Todd Vernon came out of his office. His appearance still surprised her. He didn't appear old enough to be a prosecutor, though the expensive gray suit and confident manner said differently.

"Miss White. Good to see you again." He extended his hand.

"Yes. Thank you. Mr. Vernon." Nervously, Kate accepted his hand.

He nodded and turned to her companions. "Blake and…" He tilted a questioning look toward Nichole.

"I'm Nichole." Nichole extended her own hand. "Kate's oldest friend."

"A pleasure." He gestured them toward his office. "Let's get down to business. Hold my calls please, Jane."

He ushered them inside and shut the door. At the click, Kate felt like she was doomed. Her apprehension knew no bounds.

When they were seated, Vernon pulled his chair up to his desk and leaned forward. "Let me tell you what I know." He pursed his lips. "When we catch him, the man who attacked you will be charged with trespassing, assault, aggravated assault with a deadly weapon, sexual assault with a deadly weapon, attempted rape, attempted murder and assault and battery with a deadly weapon. That's just in your case."

"What do you mean, just in *my* case?" Kate asked.

Before Vernon could respond, Nichole reached over to squeeze her hand. Troubled, she said, "None of us have had a chance to tell you, but I recognized him that night—on the computer." She paused. "Well, not exactly *recognize* because he uses disguises, but I figured out who he was when he twirled you. It was the same as what he did with the other girls—what they wrote in their diaries."

"What are you talking about?" Kate questioned.

"He's a murderer, Kate. California calls him the Red Rose Serial Killer."

Kate stared blankly at her. "Serial Killer? What…?" She lifted a hand to touch the stitches on her head and her voice trailed away.

Nichole frowned. "From the reports, the police nation-wide know who he is. His parents left him a fortune. He's said to be charming and debonair. He sweeps girls off to places like San Francisco and Boston to wine and dine them. He spends time with them, sends them flowers and then one night gives them a single red rose, rapes and murders them."

"No." Shocked tore the breath from Kate's lungs. "That stuff doesn't happen here." She covered her face with her hands. "I keep saying that. I can't believe I was so blind. Why didn't I see what he was doing? Ranae did. She tried to warn me that night. Why didn't I listen?"

"Kate, you are brave and strong. That's why you're sitting here today. You fought and you won. Nothing else matters," Nichole said.

"That's right," Vernon interjected. "But if your friends hadn't insisted that the police get involved, things might have ended differently."

"You saved my life." Kate hugged Nichole. "All of you." She reached for Blake's hand. "Thank you." She looked at Vernon. "How many are there?"

"Excuse me?"

"How many girls?"

"Kate, I'm sure you don't want to know that."

Kate shook her head stubbornly. She had to know. "I can look it up online so just tell me."

"You were the seventh that we know of."

"Seven? Oh my God." Kate bowed her head. "And I'm the only one he left alive?"

Vernon nodded.

"Dear God." She shut her eyes in silence—both in thanksgiving for her own life, and in sorrow for the girls she'd never met. "What do we do now?"

A reluctant shrug. "We can't prosecute or go forward until the police find him. In the meantime, you might want to think about going away—letting the police put you in protective custody somewhere until he's caught."

"But I graduate just a few weeks from now."

"Perhaps the college can work something out so you can graduate by proxy or something." Vernon picked up his pen to make the note.

"No." Determined. "He's not going to take that away from me, too." Kate rose.

"But honey, if your life's in danger—" Nichole began.

"Don't you see?" Kate interrupted. "If I go, he wins again. I want to graduate." There it was again, that sense that her life would never be her own again. The only thing that was helping her through was the thought of graduation. Of finishing something so she could begin something else. Start new.

"Maybe you should think about it and talk it over with your friends." Vernon came around his desk. Putting a hand lightly on Kate's shoulder he said, "We want you to be safe. Let me know what you decide."

*

Later, Kate glanced around the living room at her friends. If it wasn't for Blake being with them, the picture would look just like her memories of their high school slumber parties. On the couch, Nichole was comfy in shorts and t-shirt, her blonde hair clipped high on her head. Her long bronzed legs were crossed at the ankle and stretched across the coffee table. Nearby, Erin sat cross-legged on the floor, fiddling with the cuffs of her worn blue jeans. Her black t-shirt with the faded, "Oh Yeah, Buddy—I Care" was a perfect match for her tousled hair and just-rolled-out-of-bed look. At the opposite end of the couch from Nichole, Ranae wrapped her sweat-pant, t-shirt clad body around a throw pillow. Her long blonde hair was pulled to the side in a braid.

The odd man out, Blake had pulled a chair from the kitchen table to be part of the group. His jeans hugged his legs from his waist to the top of his boots. His button down shirt was rolled up to his forearms and unbuttoned at the neck. His hat hung on a hook in the hallway. Without it, his hair fell to the edges of his eyes, and she knew if he grinned, he would look like the seventeen-year-old boy she'd fallen in love with. But his tanned face had the curves and angles of a man. His blue eyes were sharp and patient in this moment, where they had lately been anxious. For her, Kate realized. He'd hung close since the attack, not letting her out of his sight for more than a minute.

She swallowed, trying to wrap her mind around what that might mean.

Where he sat, Blake felt Kate's eyes on him. He knew she was looking for something she couldn't yet name, so he let her look. He used the time to scan the room, noticing the subtle changes the girls had made to help themselves get over the violation of the attack on Kate. The furniture had been rearranged. There were new pillows on the couch, new pictures on the wall. New candles adorned different shelves and tables.

There was also a new throw rug in front of the rocking chair. In the darkest moments when he shut his eyes, Blake still saw the blood on the old ones. It scared him, how angry the vision made him feel, but he couldn't rid himself of it. It lay there with his rage, right below the surface of his thoughts. He was getting good at hiding it, but he knew there'd be no relief from either the vision or the wrath until Luke went down or he personally put the bastard in the ground. He looked at Kate. Seeing her huddled in the rocking chair, gripping the blanket in her lap just added another layer to his fury. He let it pile up, understanding that it would be there when he needed it and could do something about it. Calmly, he held Kate's gaze. *Yeah, that's right, darlin', you might not realize it yet, but I'm here and*

*I'm not leaving.* When she viewed him with confusion, he tilted his lips into the ghost of a smile. When her eyes widened and she looked away, he smiled fully. *Yep,* he decided, *stayin' right here...*

Ranae's voice pulled him back into the room. "So tell us what the prosecutor said."

"Mr. Vernon wants me to leave town for a while." Kate pulled on the fringe at the blanket's edge.

"What the hell for?" Erin looked at Nichole.

"He thinks Kate would be safer if she left Colorado as soon as possible. They don't have any idea where Luke is and they're afraid he'll try to come after her again."

"I won't get to graduate," Kate said miserably. "All this time and..." She swiped a tear from her cheek. "And it just feels like if I leave, he'll have taken everything from me."

"I think you should graduate." Blake sat forward in his chair. He wanted to hold her, comfort her, tell her she was safe. But any time he even tried to touch her, she jumped. He understood, but it didn't help. Not entirely. If Kate never faced her fear, she'd be terrified forever. Leaving for the sake of safety would only remove her from the security of the people she needed most if she was going to heal. "I think you should spend part of the summer with your friends and then maybe go see your mom."

Kate looked at him. Really? she silently asked.

Blake nodded.

"How's that going to work?" Nichole asked. "How are you going to keep her safe if she stays here where he can find her the minute he looks? I have to go back to L.A., damn it!"

"It's worked so far," Ranae told Nichole.

"One of us will be with Kate all the time," Erin added.

"You can't be," Nichole flung her arms out. "There'll always be that one moment when things feel better and someone gets careless and..."

Blake held up a hand to stop her worst case invective. "I'll be here," he said bluntly. "Always. Careless isn't gonna happen." He looked at Kate. "I know I've kinda just been in between places lately. Having my grandparents bring me clothes and just sort of following along with whatever you guys do, but if Kate's going to stay here and go back to work and class…" He shrugged. "I'll go with her. I don't really have to be anywhere else. And that couch is actually comfortable."

"But what about the rodeos?" Kate asked.

"What about them? They aren't more important than you."

Kate gave him a disbelieving stare.

Blake shrugged. "It's true, darlin'. So I guess if it's okay with you and Ranae, you've got yourself a permanent bodyguard."

"See, that'll be great." Ranae looked at Nichole who nodded in agreement.

"Damn right," Erin said.

*Damn* is right, Kate thought.

# CHAPTER 10

The weeks had passed and May arrived without incident. Tomorrow Kate would graduate with her friends. Tonight the evening sun poured through the window onto the ironing board in front of her. The light yellow dress draped over it was what she planned to wear under her cap and gown. On Kate's left thumb there was a Band-Aid. It was the last one; Blake had put it there that morning even though the cut was really just mostly scar. All of the cuts and most of the bruises from that night had healed, but Blake insisted. She had a sort of half-thought that he might be using this last bandage as a reminder to himself not to let down his guard, not to take the weeks of quiet for granted.

He'd been there every morning and evening, spent every day in constant vigilance, yet Kate couldn't help but think that he would leave again the way he had before. But he hadn't.

Earlier she'd made dinner for him, found herself watching for him when Ranae went out shopping. Things were starting to feel almost normal—except not quite. She'd almost overcome the constant need to have someone in the a room with her at all times. She still wanted them close by, but it was nice to be able to have Erin read her latest fashion magazine on the couch in the living room instead of at the kitchen table.

It was amazing how far she'd come when she thought about it. She used to feel her skin tingle as she walked from the bathroom to the living room where she half expected to find Luke waiting for her. She was also finally able to be alone in her own room. That was probably due, in part, to Ranae rearranging the furniture and in part to all the friends who never left her alone. That part had driven her crazy sometimes, especially when all she wanted was some peace. But it had helped to get her to where she was now, too, so she was grateful.

"Mmmm. It smells great," Blake said, opening the door and coming in.

"Hey, great." Erin walked into the kitchen and headed for the door. "You're here. I'm going to go down town and meet up with Ranae. I just saw this cute thing we need to buy."

"Good to see you too, Erin." Blake laughed.

"Bye."

Kate smiled as the door shut behind her friend. The past weeks hadn't been easy on them, either. Still smiling, she met Blake's eyes.

*God, she looks good*, he thought. There was just enough light in her smile to make him think she might really be fine. But the moment faded and the wary, injured look returned. Still, Blake had a plan. "Can we chat before we eat?"

"Sure," replied Kate. "What's going on?"

Blake put his arm around her as they sat. He was pleased that she didn't flinch. "Tell me what you dream about," Blake said. "I want to know what you want."

"I want a horse," Kate answered and didn't even try to hold back the tears. "I miss Lady Bug."

"I know, darlin'."

"I've needed her." Kate clenched her hands in her lap and let the tears slip down her cheeks. "She was there when no one else was and he took her, too."

Blake moved slow and easy. He feathered his fingertips across Kate's skin, gathering the tears as he went. "I'm sorry." His gut clenched with so many emotions, he had no idea what to do with them. So he just cupped Kate's face and watched the misery swim through her eyes while his insides knotted. "Tell me what else you want."

Kate closed her eyes. She needed this right now. Needed the understanding and the warmth. After a minute, she said, "I want to watch the sunset every night from my porch swing. I want to

hear the crickets and the caddie-dids just like when I was little."
She sighed. "I want the peace of owning land as far as my eye can
see. I want a horse that can run so fast it makes the tears slide from
my eyes. I want to teach kids who need someone to love them. I
want Erin, Ranae, and Nichole to be in my heart and my life for
years to come, and I want to be in theirs. That's it, I guess." Except
for wanting someone to share it with, she added silently. "What
do you want?"

"I want a big ranch. Bigger than the one I run with Grandpa.
I want some good horses to ride. I want a piece of ground that
will help make money for the rest of my life, and that I can leave
to my kids. I want a small stand of good water that I can fish in
and a mountain in the distance that has deer and elk. And..." He
clasped his hands in his lap. "I want someone to share it with."

Someone to share it with? "Blake, can I ask you a question?"
Kate asked softly.

"Sure. Anything." He searched her features for clues as to what
she was thinking.

"Are you mad at me?"

"No."

"Are you mad at me about Luke?" Kate paused to put her
thoughts in order. "I mean are you upset about what he did?" She
shook her head. That wasn't quite what she wanted to know.

"Darlin', I'm not angry at you about any of it. As for him..."
He hesitated, understanding what she needed to know, not sure
if he could tell her. "*Upset* isn't quite the word for how I feel. I
would've killed him that night, still could, but I couldn't leave you
then and I won't leave you now. Also," he paused, "to tell you the
truth I'm mad at myself. Furious, in fact, for not being with you."

"Do you still want to touch me?" Kate finally asked what she
really wanted to know. To try.

Blake took a deep breath. When they were in high school, when
there was no future, no Luke, and she was filled with laughter and

fun there was no one he'd wanted more. Now that she was a woman with a few scars and secrets, there still was no one he wanted more. He tried to put a hold on his desire so he wouldn't scare her with the depth and breadth of it. But Kate saw it anyway, just as soon as she asked the question. Now she waited to hear the answer.

"You're enough to kill a man with want. I want to touch you so bad it hurts. When I stand next to you, your scent makes me crazy."

"Then why don't you touch me?"

"Because sometimes when I look at you," Blake's fingers reached to caress her cheek. Kate immediately flinched. "I see the fear in your eyes."

Kate hadn't meant to flinch. She wanted to feel his touch. "I'm sorry."

"Don't be sorry. I'm not."

She looked up at him to see what he meant.

"I'm not sorry because that means when we do touch again, when we finally kiss, it will be all the more special because we had to wait for it." He almost reached out again, but stopped himself. He hated her fear. It made him furious. "There is something I have for you, though." He walked to the end of the couch and pulled a wrapped gift out of his duffle bag.

"What's this?"

"An early graduation present." He smiled.

Kate examined the package. The paper was silver with small graduation caps and tassels on it. A long green ribbon was tied around it. With scissors, she cut the ribbon and the tape away. Inside the wrapping was a beautiful cherry wood frame.

"To hold your diploma," Blake said. "I am so proud of all you have done."

"Thank you. I—" Kate began.

"I'm not finished yet," interrupted Blake, handing her another package.

This one felt odd and bulky. Kate ripped the paper this time to find a dark green horse halter. "What's this?"

"It's a horse halter." Blake winked.

"I know that. Who's it for?"

"You." He grinned.

"Why do I need it?"

"Because it goes with this." Blake handed her a picture. A small gray filly with kind eyes looked out at Kate. She stared back. "I call her Little Lady," Blake said. "She's yours. I know that you want to be a teacher. I know you'll be a wonderful one. But the part of you that's *you* is missing." He pointed at her. "It's the part of you that belongs on the back of a horse. I know that you're probably not ready to have another one just yet, but maybe you'd give Little Lady a chance. When she's a little bigger."

Kate looked stunned. "Why do you call her Little Lady?"

"Well, darlin', because she's—little." Seeing Kate fluster, Blake didn't joke, just told his story. "I contacted the owner of Lady Bug's dam and sire. For years I tried to get him to sell Lady's mom to me. He refused every price I offered. Finally, I convinced him to breed them again and to sell that foal to me. That's one of the reasons I went to Alaska. I wanted the extra cash that I needed for her to be my own and not Grandpa's. A filly was born about a year ago. Little Lady is *her*."

"You bought a horse for me?"

"Yes, darlin', I did."

The rest of what Blake said sank in. Little Lady was hers. "Blake," was all Kate could say, the tears were streaming so fast. She had so much to say, but nothing would come. *Blake bought me a horse. Not just any horse—Lady Bug's sister.* Looking at the picture, Kate could see the same eyes, the same confident look.

"Can I see her?"

"Of course you can," Blake answered elated. "Do you want to go now?"

"Yes."

\*

The drive to the ranch seemed touched with magic. The longer days of summer were coming and even with evening coming on the sun was still bright. The view of the prairie sage showing green and purple through the window on her side of the truck was spectacular. The Lazy J Ranch spread long and wide at the mountain's feet seemed even more so. The sight of the wrought iron sign with its sideways J brand of the Spencer ranch, made her smile when she remembered Leona saying of it, "Oh, hell it just means that the old man's lazy."

"How is Leona?" Kate asked as Blake's truck curved up the narrow winding dirt road to the home corrals.

"She's doing fine. I think she conned Grandpa into lettin' her buy a new pair of boots for your graduation tomorrow."

"How many does that make?" Kate laughed. She'd seen Leona's closet. Clothes were not the priority.

"One hundred and twelve."

"Are you kidding?" Kate laughed again and noticed a small pair of gray ears poke up from the end corral as Blake turned off the truck. "Can I go? Can just I go?" she asked, so wanting to meet Little Lady on her own.

"Of course." Blake walked around to open her door—But Kate was already gone. Happiness filled him as he saw Kate rush from the truck, but slow her walk to the corral as to not frighten the little horse.

"Hey, baby," Kate's voice was a whisper as she lifted the latch that held the gate to Little Lady's pen. "Come see me. Oh, you are a pretty little thing with those eyes."

The horse gave a tiny whinny as she walked to bow her head at Kate's hands.

"Well, look at that. You act like you know me. Who told you about me?" Kate wrapped her arms around the small neck, breathing in the scent of horse. "My Little Lady Bug," she crooned. "I love you already." Her hands trembled as she held the little horse. Tears filled her eyes and dripped into the dust at her feet. For an instant she gave into the desire to dream about the years to come. About training this Little Lady to carry her around the rodeo barrels.

The cool wind that accompanied the setting sun brought Kate from her dreaming in time to watch the world turn to a brushed gold while the mountains misted with purple. She remembered her last ride with her Lady Bug, and the dreams she had once held. The future wouldn't be the same without Lady Bug, but looking into the eyes of Lady's sister, the dreams she used to have weren't hard to believe in again.

# CHAPTER 11

Graduation day dawned bright and clear to a knock at the apartment door.

"Leona, what are you doing here?" Kate opened the door to see the chipper little lady with fussed over gray hair and new red-and-black boots.

"I just came to help you get gussied up for your graduation. And from the looks of it, we had better get started." Leona looked Kate over, taking in the hair that was still braided from the night before and the eyes that were puffy from being awake too long. "Up dreaming about that horse, were you?" Leona smiled.

"Yes. I guess a little."

"A little my butt, now sit down right here and let's get to work." Leona left Kate to finish her breakfast while she clunked her new boots off to the bathroom to get all the supplies she needed for doing Kate's hair. And to talk to Blake in the living room. "You get yourself on outta here and go check on those cows. This is a women's day and you don't need to be here for it."

"Good morning, Grandma." Blake winked at her from his seat on the couch.

"Well, you're the charming cowboy this morning, aren't you?" Leona patted his head. It wasn't often she could reach it. She enjoyed being able to fool herself that for just a moment he was still her boy.

"Always, Grandma. Always." Blake stood, towering over her—knowing even as he did so that there wasn't a person in the world taller than Leona. She had too much personality to ever be mistaken for small. He grinned and kissed the top of her head. "I'll see you in a while," he told Kate as he walked through the kitchen. His mood was still light, so he kissed Kate's cheek. When she didn't flinch, he whistled all the way to the truck.

"Good morning, Leona," called Ranae. "How are you? Did you get your boots?"

"Darn right I did and I'm fine." Leona smiled at Kate whose hand was on her cheek, covering the spot of Blake's kiss.

"How many pairs do you have now, Leona?" Ranae hollered.

"One hundred and twenty-four, and don't tell Jack or I'll skin ya both."

"Oh my God. I thought Kate said you only had one hundred and twelve." Ranae laughed.

"Well, that just goes to show you the men in that house don't know how to count."

Kate finally heard the conversation going on around her asked, "Where did you hide the other twelve pair, Leona?"

"Under the bed. Any housewife worth her salt knows her husband's not going to be looking under the bed for anything. Those are old anyway. I don't wear them much."

"You almost have enough to wear a different pair every day of the year," Kate declared.

"That's the plan, Darlin', that's the plan." Leona smiled. "Now quit distracting me. I'm trying to do your hair."

"Thanks, Leona."

"Don't mention it. I may not do as good as your mama would, but I can curl as good as the next gal." A tear slid down Kate's cheek. Leona patted her arm. "Now don't you go gettin' all teary eyed. I've got sympathetic tear ducts and if you start, you'll have me a bawling like a calf stuck in barb wire."

"Okay. Sorry." Kate sniffed. "It's just that I really miss her today. I have a lot lately. We were like best friends. I remember sometimes mom would call in sick to work and we'd stay up all night watching movies and talking."

"Have you told Maggie yet?" Leona asked.

"No." Kate bowed her head.

"Don't you think you ought to?"

"I've thought about it. Even talked to the girls about what to do, but I don't think I can." Kate wiped a tear away.

"You're her little girl. She has a right to know, don't you think?"

"Yeah…but I told her about Lady and that was hard enough. She's spent I don't know how many hours worrying about that. She'll go crazy if—"

"I know what you mean," Leona interrupted. "I feel the same way and you're only mine by proxy."

For the next while, Leona coaxed Kate and Ranae to tell her stories about all the things they did in college and the memories they had of growing up. It made the morning go a little faster and it helped wipe away the lingering sadness. Before they knew it, Nichole and Erin had arrived and it was time to take pictures. Leona stayed to help.

"Now, girl, you just stand there in that pretty red dress and don't sass me," Leona scolded Erin. "This is like teachin' a rattler to eat with a fork."

"How many of these damn pictures do we have to take anyway?" Erin shot back.

"Well you have to have one of all of you together in several different poses and then you all have to have one with Kate individually and then one with Ranae individually and then—"

"Ah, hell, I got it," Erin said. And sighed. Big.

"I think we should all stand in the grass outside," suggested Ranae.

"And what, get dog shit on your shoes. No," Erin growled. Her patience was nearly gone.

"I think we should all stand by this mural of Ireland Kate has on the wall," Nichole chimed in.

Kate looked at the view of the Cliffs of Moher that she'd found years before and wished she could take it with her when their lease was up.

"That'll be great," Ranae agreed and smiling, she stepped into place and put her arm around Kate.

The flashing of Kate's camera began.

Finally all that was left was the graduation itself. Looking around the basketball court turned auditorium, Kate saw advertisements on the walls for the local bars—The Pub, Wranglers and the Pig. She saw other advertisements for law offices, restaurants, and coffee shops, all of which supported the college and sought recognition for their dollars.

Her mind wandered to the previous night. It was true what she'd told Leona about lying awake, dreaming about Little Lady, but now she was thinking more about what she and Blake had talked about when they'd gotten home from the ranch.

"I wanted to say I'm sorry," Blake had told her.

"For what?"

He'd paused uncomfortably, then shrugged. "For all the things I never did. For not being there when you needed me the most." Anger had filled his features.

Kate shivered. "What?"

"I should've been the one taking you to San Francisco. Maybe not on a private jet, but I could have. We can go anywhere in the world—"

"Wait," Kate interrupted waiving her hand. "I don't want to do all that. I didn't want that when I was doing it." Tears stung eyes. *All I ever wanted was you*, she thought.

"I'm just sorry I wasn't there."

"You were when it was important." Kate remembered pausing before she said, "Can I ask you something?"

"Yes."

"Why'd you leave when Mom was in the hospital? You made sure that she got there safe, and that Nichole and I got there from the rodeo, but as soon as we did you left. Why?"

"Because I couldn't stand to see you hurt."

"I thought it was because you didn't want me anymore, but earlier you said—"

"That I didn't want you?" Blake shook his head. "Nothing could be farther from the truth. I couldn't stay because I didn't know what to do. I didn't know how to help you or how to fix the problem." He rubbed his face. "Your tears tore at me. Still do."

"Then why are you here now?"

"Because I need to be. You need me to be. And," he admitted wryly, "maybe I've grown up since the last time you saw me."

"You know I never expected you to fix the problem. I just wanted you to be there with me."

"I didn't understand that then. I was…" he hesitated, searching for the word "…selfish and I'm sorry. I just figured it was about time you heard it out loud." Again he paused.

"What?" Kate asked.

"Well, I was wondering if you'd let me hold you now? You know to sort of make up for all the times I didn't."

The request made her smile. "I guess that might be okay."

Gently, Blake had pulled her into his lap and curled his arms around her. "Thank you, darlin'," he whispered against her ear and smiled.

"Thank you, Blake." Kate had rested her head on his shoulder and closed her eyes. Maybe everything will work out, Kate hoped.

Now, waiting to graduate, Kate thought of Blake in a way she hadn't let herself since he'd walked out of her mother's hospital room and left her alone. She opened her heart and the love she'd always felt for him was still there. It was small and faded, but with each breath she took it pulsed to life again. She could feel it travel through her body, creating warmth as it went. Excitement flared and raced through her. She closed her eyes and felt Blake's hands on her face, his lips caress hers. She could see his easy, teasing grin. She could smell his strong body as he pressed it against her. She smiled.

From his spot in the stands, Blake watched Kate. He'd been watching her since he sat down. He smiled slightly when she hunched over in her seat to plant her elbows on her knees. She doesn't even know she's doing it, he thought. But then she sat up, tucked a stray hair behind her ear, folded her hands in her lap, and smiled.

He wanted to be the cause of that smile.

A big bang sounded through the gym. Both Kate and Blake jumped. Neither had noticed the commotion near the stage where the band was set up. The traditional drum "boom" caused the crowd to clap and whistle. The graduation ceremony had begun.

*

As soon as the ceremony was over, Leona headed for Blake.

"Blake, I need you." Leona grabbed his shirt and yanked him around the corner behind a huge potted fern.

"Good to see you too, Grandma," Blake teased.

"I know, sorry, but this is serious."

"What's going on?" Blake's heart almost stopped. He had never seen his grandmother's face look so pale. "Is Grandpa okay?" That would be the worst. Blake didn't even want to think such a thing.

"Yes, now be quiet and listen. I found a red rose."

"What?" The meaning quickly registered. Blake's eyes hardened. "Where?"

"This morning after I took the pictures of the girls. I was leaving the apartment to go home and I found the rose on the sidewalk by the door. I didn't know what to do. You and the girls were ready to leave. I just put the rose in the truck."

"Was there a note?"

"I didn't see one."

"Did you tell Grandpa?"

"Yes."

"Don't tell Kate."

"No, of course not today."

"Not ever."

"Don't you think she should know?"

"Don't you think she should know what?" Kate asked as she walked up.

"Oh, damn," Leona said. "I didn't want to spoil the surprise."

"What surprise?" Kate smiled.

"Oh, nothing except, we have this great big cake and balloons and music and people and food. You know a party, for you and the girls." Leona put her arm around Kate's shoulder and led her away.

"Really? We were just going to—"

"Nonsense. We have it all planned."

Good cover, Grandma, Blake thought.

Leona looked back at him and gave him the you-do-it look.

Oh, hell. I guess I'd better call the ranch and have some food made. How in the world am I going to find a cake and balloons on graduation weekend in this town? Blake walked toward his truck, pulling his phone out of his pocket.

First things first, he thought grimly and called Aaron Barrs.

# CHAPTER 12

Before the lease ended on Kate and Ranae's basement apartment, Ranae had searched for a house to buy. She'd found a beautiful little white one-bedroom on the edge of town. Boxes of clothes and books and all the things Kate thought she would need in Oregon were packed and stacked in the corner of Ranae's living room. Kate was sleeping on her couch. This was the last weekend she and the girls would share before Kate left for Oregon. They'd decided to spend some of it at the rodeo.

"Blake, will you just let me go first?" Kate asked. They were sitting in Blake's truck parked behind the arena. "It's early, but I want to—"

"Go ahead, darlin'." Understanding what she meant, what she needed—to feel the excitement and nervousness that every participant experienced before the rodeo's start—Blake unlatched Kate's seatbelt and squeezed her hand. "I'll be right here if you need me." He knew he had to let her go, give her back the independence that her attacker had taken from her, but all he wanted to do was call Chief Barrs again to verify that Luke wasn't in the area. He'd talked to Barrs once a week since graduation and there was still no sign of Kate's would-be killer/rapist or even how the rose had been delivered. That fact made Blake more worried than relieved. It felt like waiting for a rattler to strike.

On a grateful smile, Kate stepped out of the truck. She was greeted by rodeo sounds, sights and smells. All around her tack compartments slammed and horse trailer gates squeaked. The low hum of contestant voices filtered to her as they went through the motions of preparing for the rodeo. Cowboys warmed up roping arms or stretched in anticipation of the rough stock ride ahead. Some wore shirts that hadn't been washed since the first time the cowboy had ridden to a win or close to one, hoping the luck would find them. In other areas, cowgirls warmed up their horses or glossed their mouths with lipstick or fastened on their lucky earrings. The whole affair, all the careful acts and routines, were rituals sacred to the doer.

"Getting their head right," Kate whispered as her feet moved the first few steps. She remembered the green ribbon that was attached to her saddle horn. Her mom had tied it there herself. "For luck, for safety—for winning," Maggie had said smiling.

Of all the rodeo grounds she knew from New Mexico to Kansas, from Wyoming, Montana to Utah, this one here in Colorado was her favorite. It was her hometown rodeo. It was where she'd carried her first flag. As rodeo queen, it was where she waved to the crowds for the first time. As a professional barrel racer, she'd made her first run in this dirt. It was good dirt, damp and heavy, sturdy enough to withstand the fury of horse hooves as they pounded around the barrels.

Among all the chatter and laughter and shuffling of hooves, there was a serious mood. With each passing rodeo, the time until the season's end grew shorter, the competitions more determined. There were only six months left until the Finals. Every second, every turn of rope, every powerful jump of a rodeo bronc became more important. Kate could feel the anxiousness. As she walked among the contestants many hollered a hello or gave a whistle. She waved back, but didn't stop to talk. They didn't have time right now to chat or break concentration. As she curved around a horse trailer with New Mexico plates she saw a girl struggling with her hat.

"Can I help?" Kate asked.

"I don't know. I can't seem to keep it clean and I can't seem to keep it on, when I run the barrels." The girl's eyes were a striking blue against her pale face.

Kate laid a hand against the girl's shaking ones. "I know a secret. White hats are beautiful and hard to keep clean. But," Kate winked, "if you sprinkle them with baby powder the dark smudges disappear."

"Okay. I have some that I use on my cinch once in a while." The girl smiled.

"Well there you go. Now as to keeping your hat on." Kate pointed to the other horse trailers parked nearby. "I'm sure that one of the girls along here has a few extra hat pins." The girl's confused look made Kate smile. "They're just really long, sturdy bobby pins. And so you don't get a headache, put the flat side against your head."

"How'd you know all that?"

"Oh, I know a thing or two about barrel racing. My name's Kate." She held out her hand.

"Kate?" The girl reached for Kate's hand. "Kate White!"

Kate nodded.

The girl giggled. "I'm shaking Kate White's hand. I'm Rebecca Connar."

"Hello Rebecca. You're from Santa Fe, aren't you?"

"Yeah. How'd you know that?"

"Oh, well. You know things." Kate smiled.

Rebecca let go of Kate's hand. "I heard about what happened to your horse. I'm sorry."

"Yeah, she was awesome." Kate looked at Rebecca's horse. "Your Buster's pretty awesome too."

"I love him." Rebecca paused. "Hey Kate?"

"Yeah?"

"If I win tonight, I'm going to dedicate it to you and your Lady Bug."

Tears filled Kate's eyes. "That'd be great," she whispered.

Walking toward the arena, Kate took a deep breath. The scents of the rodeo grounds filled her lungs. Dust kicked up by the rodeo stock. Freshly popped popcorn. Bubblegum cotton candy. Manure. Sweat. Diesel fuel. All the aromas swirled together in the breeze, telling her more clearly than words, *it's a hot summer night in June and it's rodeo time!* Crossing her arms on a fence rail and laying her chin on her wrist, Kate leaned into the tall, blue steel posts and rails surrounding the wide arena. Closing her eyes, she let the soft wind bring the memories. Soon she was holding Lady's reins and balancing with the horse's powerful body as they rounded the barrels and made the dirt fly.

"Sometimes I feel like I'm only half a person without you, Lady Bug."

Blake heard the muffled statement and his heart cried with Kate. He'd been sitting in the truck watching her. He'd smiled as she walked by the cowboys and cowgirls getting ready for the night and their various greetings. He'd laughed when he saw the young girl jump up and down with excitement when she realized who Kate was. He'd begun to believe that coming tonight was a good idea. Now, he wasn't so sure seeing tears slip from beneath Kate's closed eyes and flow down her cheeks.

"Hey, darlin'." Blake leaned against the railing beside her.

Kate opened her eyes and looked at Blake. His eyes fiercely held hers. She desperately wanted to be the way she used to be. The last time he'd looked at her with that look was the last time he'd kissed her. Really kissed her, not the little ones he gave her every day now, but really kissed her. She remembered how he'd grabbed her off the ground and how her body felt crushed against his. How his lips had been hot and wanting. How she'd felt needed and womanly and perfect. Now she felt wounded and empty. The tears kept falling.

Blake reached to brush them away. Her hands closed over his as he smoothed his fingers across her face, catching her tears. Her warmth traveled through his body. *God she's beautiful,* he thought. The sunlight streamed through her hair, setting it afire. Her green eyes, though filled with tears, held passion. He so wanted to gather her to him and kiss away the fear, the pain and sadness. He wanted to make her forget that there was ever anything, but him.

"Do you want to go home?"

"No, Blake." *I want you.* Kate's eyes pleaded with him. *Can't you see? I want you?*

He studied her for a moment trying to figure out what she was thinking. What she meant by the tone in her voice. But decided that what he saw in her eyes couldn't be there. Wouldn't be. So he linked his fingers with hers. "Let's go find the girls then."

The girls were sitting in the middle of the grandstands, directly in front of the bucking chutes. They weren't hard to see. Most all of the other spectators had cowboy hats, jeans, button up shirts and boots on. But the girls wore sandals, shorts and t-shirts. As Blake and Kate got closer, they could hear them laughing.

"Hey, guys, look at that." Nichole pointed toward Blake and Kate.

"Holy shit," Erin muttered. "They're holding hands."

"I think it's sweet," Ranae said, munching up a piece of popcorn.

"Yeah, you would. Miss romance. Barf, barf." Erin smiled.

Nichole nodded. Seeing Blake with Kate was sweet. But it was more, too. It was the way it was supposed to be. If any two people were supposed to be together, it was Blake and Kate.

"I'm glad to see it." Nichole grabbed some of Ranae's popcorn.

"Hey! I paid for that." Ranae snatched back the bag.

"You know we all can get a bag," Blake teased as he and Kate walked up.

"Well, look who's just in time to wait a half an hour before the rodeo begins." Erin looked at her watch. "You're going to have to tell me again why the hell we came so early."

"To get the best seats." Kate sat down beside Ranae and dug into the popcorn.

"Geez. Does this say free or what." Ranae smiled and hugged Kate. "You look good," she whispered.

"Thanks." Kate felt much better.

As the grand entry left the arena, they all stood. One big black horse remained with a rider who held a huge American flag. It whipped in the sharp breeze of the evening. As a strong, clear-voiced girl began to sing the National Anthem, Blake remembered his and Kate's first real rodeo. Sure they'd competed in high school rodeos and the local amateur ones as well, but this one was the first big one. They both had their professional rodeo cards tucked inside their pocket, filling it and their hearts with gold buckle dreams. That competition was in the arena that stretched out before him.

In his mind he could see himself as he stood, hat over his heart, with his boots hooked in the bars of the chute above the back of his ride. He could feel Kate's good luck kiss drying in the breeze of the evening. While he waited for the anthem to be done and the rodeo to begin, he thought of the greatest honor in his life, that he could slip on his riding glove, press his hand into his riggin' and come together with a beautiful, powerful animal.

Horse and rider each had a job to do, one they both loved. The horse got to explode into an arena filled with dirt and sky. The rider got to feel an unparalleled sense of freedom as the horse made that first jump out of the chute. For eight seconds he got to be the man he'd heard about in songs, the man who'd won the west, the man who was the pride of a country. For those few seconds he got to live every little boy's dream. And it didn't matter that during those seconds his back was wrenched, his arm yanked or his head battered. All that mattered was when he heard the buzzer, he was that man—the American Cowboy.

In memory, those lofty thoughts disappeared when the chute boss hollered, "Spencer, you're up!"

Nodding, Blake shimmied down in the chute next to the buckskin mare. "Well, old girl, how about giving this cowboy a break."

"Not damn likely," came a voice from the edge of the chute.

Blake had looked up to see a face he'd seen in every professional rodeo magazine for the previous couple of years. The man with a kid's grin, sooty gray eyes and a blazing green shirt was this year's world champion bareback rider.

"A guy can hope," Blake remembered smiling at one of his heroes.

"You're gonna feel like the devil's calling roll on that first jump. She won't slow down either. She'll go to the right first damn thing. If you stick with her, watch the fence. She likes to plant cowboys for a hobby."

Blake recalled how the fear that started out as a little ball of annoyance in the pit of his stomach grew. He'd drawn the horse maybe five guys had managed to ride that year. Pulling his fingers on his left hand through the grip of his riggin' and squeezing his body as close to it as possible, Blake fought the fear. Rosin sticking, hand tight Blake raised his feet above the horse's shoulders and laid his back against the body of his ride. He felt the heat. Smelled dirt and horse mix with his own sweat. Blake nodded and said, "Outside!"

The chute gate slammed open.

For a second that seemed to last an eternity, nothing happened. But all the silence was just the build up for the explosion. The anxiety wound so tight in Blake's arm and back and body when the horse did make that first jump, he was ready. Snorting, rearing the mare barreled out of the chute with all the strength of a cannon. Her excitement was contagious. It flowed up Blake's arm and thrilled his whole body into motion. This was the part she loved. She could fling that man who thought he could hold on with just one hand to dirt anytime she pleased. And that was the plan, she just wanted to have fun for a bit. Breathing the air, kicking the sky she bucked and twisted in the dust.

Blake could see the ground, the clouds, the stands, his boots, his chaps. But he had no idea if the mare had jumped to the right, to the left or to the moon. All he knew was that he had a firm grip and that his legs were still moving. Every leap the mare took yanked his arm and lashed his head. He felt beaten, pulverized. He felt free, alive. Dimly, he heard the buzzer and the cheering crowd, and he let go.

Gathering himself out of the dirt, waiving to the crowd and walking back to the chutes was the proudest moment of his life. The gold buckle that had graced his belt at the end of that year and the handshake he received from the man with a kid's grin, saying, "Congratulations Champ," almost compared.

The last strain of the National Anthem and the crowd's cheering brought Blake back to the present. He looked over at Kate. She was watching him. She knew what he'd been thinking. Smiling, she squeezed his hand a little tighter.

Pulling her program from the seat behind her, Kate sat down. She glanced at the cover and the world went blurry.

Blood red letters defiled the picture of the barrel racer on the cover. "Are you dreaming, Kate?" it read.

He was back.

# CHAPTER 13

"Darlin', look at that rodeo clown, he's—" Blake looked at Kate. His heart pounded when he saw the terrified look on her face. He knew in a second what the cause of it was. He grabbed the program out of her hand. "Where did you get this? *Kate!*"

Too panicked to hear him, she didn't answer.

"Mister, what'd she win?" A voice asked.

Blake glanced over his shoulder to the girl with shiny silver braces behind him. "What?"

"What'd she win?"

"Nothing." Blake turned back to Kate. "Where did you get this?"

"A man traded with her. Said he had to go, but that he had a winning program. He said he wanted someone to win since he wasn't—"

"What'd you say? What man?"

"The man who traded programs." The girl rolled her eyes.

"Which way did he go? What'd he look like?"

"He left." She pointed to the bottom of the grand stands. "He looked like a surfer from California. Probably decided he didn't like the rodeo. He was wearing sandals like some weirdo."

"It was Luke," Kate said trying to keep her voice from shaking. "I know it was."

"He didn't tell me his name." The girls stuffed a large wad of cotton candy in her mouth. "So what'd you win?"

"Where you from?" Blake asked.

"Montana."

"Where's your family?"

"My dad's Chris Bauer. He's in the rodeo tonight." The girl's eyes lit with pride.

"Blake, I called Chief Barrs. He's on his way to the station now.

We'd better go." Nichole said.

"Right." Blake helped Kate to her feet then turned to the girl. "You find your father or friends he trusts to look after you when he rides and stay with them. Tell him not to let you out of his sight, you hear me?" He pointed an imperious finger toward the rodeo arena.

The girl rolled her eyes at him. "I can take care of myself."

"No," Blake assured her. "This time you can't." He waited for her to go.

She stared at him rebelliously for another moment before stepping up to make her way out of the stands. "Grown-ups are stupid," she muttered. But when the bronc chute swung open, she smiled and hurried off to get closer view of her hero's—her dad's—ride.

*

Kate had never been inside a police station before. The cold, white walls and orange chairs bolted to the concrete floor were not exactly what she'd expected. Cigarette smoke residue, stale coffee and the cinnamon gum Chief Barrs was chewing filled her nose.

"I sent a patrol to the rodeo to search for the guy you described. But—"

"But you don't think you'll find him." Blake scrubbed his face with his hands.

"No. We'll find him. It'll just take time. I suggest Kate go to Oregon as soon as possible."

"She and Blake are going next weekend," Nichole said from her seat next to Kate.

"Maybe you can leave earlier. I think we'd all feel better if you were out of Colorado."

"Should she fly? That's faster." Ranae stood.

Barrs hunched a shoulder. "I don't really know if 'faster' is best in this instance. We don't know what sort of connections Luke has. If he has the kind I think he might, he'll be able to search the passenger lists for your name. In that case, keeping him off balance by getting there another way might be best."

"Okay," Kate said. She couldn't think right now. Whatever they decided was good as long as it kept everyone out of harm's way.

"Maybe I could see if my brother could fly in from Chicago. He's a big shot with an airplane," Erin said.

"I don't want you to do that." Kate shook her head.

"Does Luke know about your mom? Did you ever mention her to him?" Barrs asked.

"No." Kate shook her head. Then she blanched. "Wait, oh God, yes. Mom. I told him she's sick—" Kate jumped out of her chair. "She's all alone! I forgot that we talked about her—about visiting her." She raised frightened eyes first to Barrs then to Blake. "I never even thought about it. What if something happens to her?"

"Darlin', hold on." Blake grabbed a hold of her hand. He cursed Luke when she flinched. "She has a neighbor lady who goes over once a day, right?"

Anguish filled Kate's voice. "But that's not good enough. Can't the cops out there do something?"

"Of course we'll contact them," Barrs assured her at the same time that Blake said, "Your mom's neighbor is a private investigator with a background in protection work."

"She's like a bodyguard?"

"That's what I hired her for."

"You hired her?" Kate stumbled.

"Yes." Blake was relieved to see the frantic emotion leave Kate's eyes.

"I don't know what to say." She had no idea that Blake would even think of such a thing, much less do it. She was angry at herself for not thinking of it. She'd just been so busy trying to get through the last few months without worrying her mother that the idea of Luke going after her mother to get to her hadn't entered her head.

"Say thanks." Blake smiled.

"Thanks, Blake." Kate smiled uncertainly at him, but at the edge of her mind she wondered why he hadn't discussed it with her. She'd naïvely allowed Luke to use similar tactics—assumption, arrogance, and confidence—to sway her into going out with him in the first place. To suddenly understand that Blake used the same tactics on her, too, was discomfiting.

"Well you guys have a lot of work to do. I'm going to take this over to forensics." Barrs picked up the clear plastic bag containing the rodeo program. "I hope this will give us more than the other messages did," he said as the door shut behind him.

More of that discomfiting wariness washed over Kate. She backed away from Blake. "What other messages?"

*Damn.* He should have told her—should have realized that wanting to protect her from the knowledge that Luke was still hunting her, and had been since the night Blake thwarted his attack, was a really bad idea. He pursed his lips, already anticipating the fight. "There was note a left outside the apartment the night you were in the emergency room and then a rose was left in the same spot the day of graduation."

"Why didn't you tell me?"

"I wanted you to have a chance to get better." He patted her hand.

Tactical error, huge mistake. He knew it the moment the unintentionally condescending words and placating gesture were out.

"Don't treat me like a little kid." Kate grabbed her hand back. "You lied to me. Why? Don't you think I'm capable of thinking for myself? Hiring a bodyguard for *my* mom is something you should have let me help you do. I know her better than anyone." Kate couldn't prevent the anger, hurt and sense of betrayal from building. "But that. Keeping that from me in order to *protect* me? That was stupid. Why?" All the feelings she had when he'd left her and Nichole standing at the side of her mother's hospital bed came rushing back. "Damn you, Blake. Why do you always have to make me feel this way?" Kate damned herself for the furious, hot tears streaking down her face.

Blake looked at her with shocked eyes.

"Why?" Kate yelled. "Do you think I'm stupid? Or weak?" A thought occurred to her and she spit the condemnation at him. "Oh, wait. Maybe you think I'm too *fragile* to handle things I might need to know *in order to protect myself!*" Fury rushed through her like an ice flow. "Is that it? You thought I was *too fragile* to survive knowing what he wants to do to me now?"

Bleakly, Blake shook his head.

"Answer me, damn it! Is it?" Kate walked to the door and ripped it open. "Well, I'll tell you one thing. I don't need you. I don't need you to think I'm stupid or weak or helpless at all. I'm leaving."

"Kate, wait. Let's talk about this." Blake walked toward her.

"Now. You want to talk about it now. No way. I'm through talking to you." Kate turned to Nichole. "Can you take me back to the house?"

"Okay." Nichole glanced apologetically at Blake. It wasn't just Blake who'd lied. They all had.

Maybe later they could tell her.

Maybe.

Nichole glanced *coming?* at Ranae who grabbed Erin's arm and dragged her after Kate, too.

*

A short time later, tears ran down Kate's cheeks as she struggled with the zipper on her over-stuffed suitcase. She wanted to just throw all her clothes away. She'd never wear the Wranglers or the button up shirts or her boots again. But she couldn't bring herself to put her rodeo clothes in the trash. They were the only link she had left to the past she'd loved.

The damning thoughts piled up while she worked. *Why did Blake lie to me? Why did he have to do this now? We were doing so good...*

The tears she cried as she finished packing were filled with anger, sorrow, and fear.

It was long past sunset when she struggled across the yard to her car. She jammed the suitcase into the trunk, not caring that she smashed the boxes already in there. Praying that the trunk stayed closed, she banged it shut. It still seemed odd to her to have a car and not her truck and horse trailer. But after Lady Bug, she sold both and bought the seen-better-days heap. The clutch was touchy, the passenger side window wouldn't roll down and the only door that would open from the inside was the driver's. Still, the engine was new so she figured she should have no problem making the trip.

"Here's the last of the boxes, Kate," Nichole said. She held out a box that had *rodeo stuff* printed in black marker across the top.

"Where do you want these?" Ranae asked, coming out with a similar box.

"In the back seat." Kate motioned.

Erin put hers in last and said, "I'm sorry, Kate. We didn't want to keep those messages from you, but—"

"You guys knew, too?" Kate turned to face them. "Why didn't you tell me?

Ranae and Nichole bowed their heads, but Erin kept her eyes on Kate.

"Before you start yelling at us about how we lied to you and kept you from making decisions, you need to know something. You didn't see *you* after that sonofabitch steamrollered you, but we did. We saw the blood and the tears and the damn cuts on your body. I don't know how you made it through the night without breaking, but you did." Erin swiped the tears from her face. "There was no damn way in hell we were going to tell you about any note that night. And we couldn't tell you about the one on graduation day and ruin it for you. No way. I'd have punched anybody who ruined that day for you, especially that bastard Luke, but he wasn't within reach. So I don't care how mad you get." Erin waved her hand in the air. "We had a reason for what we did and if I had to do it over, I'd do the same damn thing! Because sometimes being a friend means you protect. And we were protecting you."

Kate eyed her friends. She understood their desire to protect her from… *him*, but not the fact that all they'd done was delay telling her what she *really* needed to know.

Ranae stepped a little closer to Kate. "I'm sorry you're mad at us. But none of us wanted you to hurt more than you already were."

Nichole nodded. "We don't want you to hurt now."

"Why?" Kate asked. "In all this time, why didn't one of you say something instead of hovering all the time. I'm the one who was assaulted, not you. I'm the one who has to live with that reality. It doesn't matter how close we were, or what you *felt* or what you wanted to do for me. Luke didn't try to kill you, he tried to murder *me*. I needed to know."

"Not if it would have kept you in hiding or from getting your courage back or even just healing," Erin stated flatly.

Nichole smiled tentatively. "We just wanted you *back*," she said. "We wanted to hear you laugh and joke again." She looked away. "And there was so much time between notes that we hoped—"

Kate interrupted her. "So none of you think I'm weak, stupid or helpless?"

"Hell, no. I know you're not," Erin said.

"We love you," Ranae said.

"Well, I wonder what Blake's reason is then," Kate said more to herself than to the girls.

Erin kicked at the dirt in the driveway.

Kate opened the car door. "Well, I guess I'll go."

"Kate…" Ranae put a hand on her arm.

Kate looked at her.

"Don't you think it would be better if…" She hesitated. "If someone traveled with you? Just in case?"

"Yeah," Nichole said. "Don't you want to at least wait until morning?"

"No." Kate shook her head. "I need to get out of here. I need a new start." Tears streamed down her face again. "Oregon is as good a place as any."

"What if Luke follows you, or is already there somewhere waiting for you?" Erin asked bluntly.

"Then I guess I'll deal with it, won't I?" Kate told her stubbornly.

"But…"

Again Kate shook her head vehemently. "No," she said. "No more 'buts.' It's time for me to go."

In the dim haze of the yard light Kate looked at the girls. Her friends. She tried to memorize a small bit of each one. How they looked and what they wore. Nae's smile, her loving eyes. Nichole's hair, the way it swayed in the breeze. Erin's laugh, how it always made her feel good. Kate wished that this day had never come. She wished for the days they'd already lived. Maybe they would've taken more time to cherish them. Maybe they would've laughed a little more. Maybe their trips for ice cream and their weekends out would've lasted a little longer. They had so many memories and so many good times and so much love. But, this is how I'll remember them, Kate thought. In the darkness of midnight, in the golden light they're here with me, one last time.

She slid into the car.

"I love you," she mouthed.

"We love you, too." Huddling together, the girls wrapped their arms around each other.

"I'll miss you."

"Shit. This is too much shit," Erin said.

"Knock it off." Ranae elbowed Erin.

Kate laughed. Heart aching, she closed the car door and switched over the motor. Feeling like her friends were slipping into the past, she drove away from Ranae's house.

*

Pulling into the parking lot of Waldman Stables, Kate turned off the ignition. She didn't have to get out of the car. She didn't need to go to the practice pen to remember why she came. She was really here so she could find a way to say good-bye. The real places, the ones in Kansas, Montana and Wyoming, the rodeo grounds, Kate's heart was not quite strong enough to travel to. She did remember though. She remembered when she was in Miles City, Montana. The sky had poured and a little curly haired girl with sticky fingers had given her some watermelon cotton candy. That night after the rodeo Kate met an old rodeo clown who was retiring. He was at his last rodeo.

"You can just call me Willie." His dark eyes shining with humor as he held out his hand. "My mom wanted me to be a doctor. Thought Wilson sounded like one, nah. I think Willie sounds like a cowboy, so that's me."

Willie, dressed in regular clothes looked like a cowboy. His hands were gnarled with hard work and courage and just a little bit of white paint still hung to his cheek. All the lives of all the cowboys he'd saved were felt by each sore muscle. When he found out that Kate had driven all the miles on her own over the last year and a half, he had called her bronc-y, gutsy and beautiful. "A man couldn't ask for any more than that, any cowboy's dream." He'd added with a smile that made more lines on his sun worn face.

Willie the rodeo clown had the life that Kate dreamed of. Chasing cans and the white

lines on the highway were those dreams. She loved her horse. The sleepy miles and the cold cans of pork n' beans were really just a small part of all she had wanted. There was peace there and just a little magic.

What was that poem from college—"A Dream Deferred"? That's what she felt like—the sorrow of feeling all the moments when life's dreams went still.

"Well, I'd better get on the road," Kate said to her empty car and turned the key.

The white lines didn't look the same to her from behind the wheel of a car, but they were what she had to hold onto, so she embraced them.

# CHAPTER 14

"She's gone." Sleepy-eyed, Ranae viewed Blake through the porch screen.

"What do you mean, 'she's gone'?" Without an invitation, Blake opened the door.

"Come in," Ranae said as pointedly as her groggy mind would let her. "She left last night."

"What! Damn it. I knew I should've come over here right away. I stayed to finish at the police station and then figured she'd need some time too cool off."

"She'll have plenty of time now," Ranae mumbled.

In response, Blake only scanned the neatly arranged couch, coffee table and lamp stands. There wasn't a shred of Kate anywhere. *Damn.* He slumped onto the end of the couch and buried his face in a convenient throw pillow. God, I can smell her, he swore. Damning his pride, he let the pain come. So this was what being left behind felt like. Empty, alone, lonely. No wonder Kate was still wary around him even after all this time. God, he'd blown it!

"Blake?" Ranae stood at the edge of his vision.

"Yeah." He looked up.

If Ranae hadn't been so scared, she might have noted the angry desperation in Blake's eyes. As it was, she didn't notice. "Look. I found this on the step." Hands trembling, Ranae showed him the note.

*Where are you going, Kate? Don't worry, I'll find you!* was scrawled in shaky lettering.

"Damn. I'd better call Barrs."

"Isn't there anything the rest of us can do?" Fear made Ranae's voice squeak.

"Stay out of the bastard's way so he doesn't take Kate's leaving out on you," Blake told her. Then swore. "Ah, hell, I really needed that extra week to make this work." He pulled on his hat. "You find Erin and Nichole. Then you stay in touch. No telling what he'll do when he realizes he can't find Kate."

*

When Kate reached the Oregon border, she began to see evidence of what her new life would look like.

The long, hot drive across the desert had been helpful at calming her down. The first eight hundred or so miles she'd felt like turning around. The sense of loneliness and loss had been acute. But as Oregon got closer and closer she resigned herself to the decision she'd made. Also, besides seeing her mom, she had her new life as a teacher to look forward to—of learning with her students. True, she didn't have a teaching position yet, but it would come.

Beside the road a lake of soft, placid blue stretched out before a mountain peak still capped with snow. The water looked inviting. She saw a few people fishing. Others were enjoying the bike path that edged the lake. Slowing the car and rolling down her window, Kate felt a soft breeze sift through her hair. Ducks called and children laughed. She could smell the musty, sweet smell of too much rain and not enough sun. But the sun was out today. Kate smiled, taking it as a sign of good fortune.

Another sign that her luck was holding happened when she found her mother's house. The road that led to it wound this way and that, meandering through dense forest with dozens of tiny go-nowhere offshoots. Located just north of Cottage Grove, Oregon, the route had seemed easy on paper, but the actual act of getting *there* was much more difficult—and often misleading if you didn't know exactly where you were going. She doubted very much that a GPS system had been invented that could locate it, even if satellite reception had been good. Which it wasn't.

Pulling into the drive beneath a towering walnut tree, Kate hurried to shift the car into first, pull the emergency brake and jump out. She smiled as she trotted to the front steps of a wood cottage snuggled into a protective hollow of trees. The tree limbs seemed to reach their welcoming arms around the house and out to Kate. Deep in the forest green blanketed everything around the large, arched entryway.

"Oh, Mama," Kate whispered. "It's beautiful. I should've known you'd pick somewhere like this."

Kate's foot was inches away from the front stoop, when she heard a voice behind her.

"Excuse me. Can I help you?"

Kate turned and saw a woman striding toward her. The first thing Kate noticed was her hair. The long, streaming curls of golden blonde ended at her waist. Her eyes were the next thing Kate focused on. They were a deep, searching blue. Kate felt like every inch of her was picked apart and evaluated in the span of a few seconds.

"I—my—mom. My mom lives here." Kate stood firm. Only chastising herself a little for stumbling over her tongue.

"That would make you?"

"Her daughter. I'm Kate."

"Of course you are. I would have recognized you anywhere." The woman's face changed from deep concentration to welcome. "I just had to hear you say it." She held out her hand. "I'm Sally Knox."

"You're my mom's neighbor." Kate shook her hand and was not at all surprised to feel the healthy grip.

"Yup."

"How far away do you live?" Kate asked as she looked through the trees to see if she could see another house; she couldn't.

"Not far. I saw you pull in." Sally flicked her hair back from her face. She didn't mention the network of surveillance cameras that had helped her do exactly that. "We weren't expecting you until next Saturday or Sunday. Well, I guess, I should say, I wasn't. Maggie, now she had different ideas. She said you'd be coming today." Blake had called Sally earlier that day, but she didn't know how much she was supposed to let on, so she left it at that. "We've been cooking up a storm."

"That's my mom," Kate said, studying Sally. She wondered what it would be like to be a bodyguard in secret.

"Why don't you go on in? Last time I checked she was taking a nap."

Kate nodded and crossed the porch. The wooden door slowly swished against the carpet as Kate, stepped inside. In her imagination the house she was stepping into wasn't this Hansel and Gretel cottage. It was the home she'd lived in before her mom got sick. If Kate tried, if she closed her eyes, she could smell the warm scent of bread baking and hear her mom singing somewhere in the house.

This house, however, was cool and quiet. A stream of light from the late evening sun glanced through the windows. Kate stood a moment, letting her eyes adjust to the dimness.

"Mama, where are you?" she called softly.

"Dolly, is that you? Are you here?" The soft response came from the living area.

"Yeah. Mom. It's me." Kate crossed the distance and knelt on the carpet before the couch. "I finally made it."

Reaching out a hand, Maggie felt blindly for Kate's face. Her eyes, like so many other bits of her body, had stopped working. She did all of her "seeing" now with the hands that had once had been worn with calluses and cracked by the alcohol she used as a nurse. The calluses were gone now, smoothed down by time and the medicated lotion the doctor had given her. Tears slipped down Maggie's face as she allowed herself to see her little girl.

"I'm sorry about Lady Bug. I wanted to come back and be there with you."

"I know, Mama. But the girls were there. That made it easier."

Maggie's voice was hoarse with emotion. "I never meant to leave you. I always wanted to stay, to help you study, to rejoice with you when you won. I wanted to stay."

"I know." Kate's own tears flooded her cheeks.

"We're together now. I know that it won't be the same, but maybe it'll be better. I can be home all the time and you won't have to wonder if I'll work long hours. I'll just be here and you can be with me anytime."

"I'll be with you any time I can be," Kate promised both her mother and herself. "I'm excited to be the teacher I always wanted to be. I'm glad that I get to share this with you.

"Me, too. You already have a ton of mail."

"Really?" Kate heard the uncertainty that crept into her voice. If that bastard Luke had found and sent notes to her mother...!

"What's the matter?"

"I was nervous," Kate blurted, not quite lying. Surely her mother's bodyguard would have noticed if anything was amiss with the mail. "I didn't know how this would go. Still don't, but I do feel better. I'm glad you aren't upset that I decided to stay and finish school and to rodeo in Colorado instead of coming to Oregon with you."

"Upset? Why would I be upset? We discussed it. You were where I wanted you to be. You were living your life and fulfilling part of your dreams, just like I taught you. I'm more proud of you because you did stay than if you'd have felt like you needed me and came here. I was the one who needed help, but I wouldn't have let you. I wanted you to live your life. I've lived mine and had to live with the choices I made. Some of those choices have brought me you, but some of them weren't so good. But I wouldn't change them. I love you for how brave you are."

"I don't feel brave at all. I feel scared and unsure about all of this. You would think I'd have gotten used to change by now with everything that's happened, but this is still pretty scary. I wanted to help you so badly. I felt like I hadn't done what I was supposed to do because I didn't come with you. I felt like I was doing what you would have wanted me to do if you were well and could say that you wanted me to finish school in Colorado. Living my life was important to me too, because I thought it would make you proud." Kate smiled at her mom who was now sitting up on the couch.

"Of course it does. I love you and can hardly wait to see your classroom and meet your kids. Wonder if they'll like an old blind lady?" Maggie was smiling.

"Of course they will. I'll make certain of it, because to me you aren't an old blind lady. You're my beautiful mom."

"We should call in Sally. I'm sure she's out there someplace. She's probably starving and sick of standing outside."

"Okay."

Returning to the house after getting Sally, Kate noticed all the little touches that her mom had done to make her arrival feel like a homecoming. The voice of her favorite country music singer filled the background. A long span of plush blue carpet was sprinkled with little green and silver graduation hats. Green and silver balloons hugged the kitchen ceiling while banners hung from it. One banner said *Happy Graduation* and the other one said *Welcome Home*. More confetti was sprinkled on the kitchen linoleum. The table held a chocolate frosted cake that Kate knew would be yellow inside. A huge bowl of potato salad sat beside it and thickly sliced watermelon lined a platter. Kate could also smell barbequed chicken being kept warm in the oven along with the corn on the cob. Plates were set out with silverware on the counter. Napkins were folded nicely.

"Wow! I can't believe I missed all of this when I came through!" Kate shook her head.

"Maggie said your college colors were green and white, but all I could find was the silver," smiled Sally as they all sat down at the table.

"I made the potato salad just like you like it. Extra eggs and very little pickles," added Maggie.

"I love it. Thank you so much."

"We made up the extra room for you. You know you can stay here," Maggie said as she passed the plate of chicken.

"I know I can. But—" Kate swallowed, unsure of how much her mother knew about what had happened beyond Lady Bug's untimely death. The urge to protect Maggie from everything that had happened cut deep. "I really want to have a place of my own. I don't know. I guess I feel like I need to take this next step on my own." She looked at her mom. She didn't want to hurt her feelings, but she was sure she probably had. What she saw surprised her.

Maggie was smiling. "Dolly, I know you want to do this. But I'm your mother. I still have a right to hope, don't I? And besides I'm proud of you for taking such a big step."

"Thanks." Kate took a bite of her chicken and realized she was definitely hungry.

"Sounds good." Across from Kate, Sally filled her fork with potato salad and made a mental note to call Blake and tell him that Kate wouldn't be living in Maggie's spare bedroom.

# CHAPTER 15

"I need a few more days before I can leave here," Blake told Ranae and Erin unhappily as they sat over beers at The Pub. "I can't leave without someone acting as foreman at our place while we're gone." He shoved his hands through his hair in frustration. "I've got someone to step in, but he needs to get things squared away on his end. Even for this, I can't leave my grandparents without help."

"The police near Kate's mom have been notified about the threats, right?" Erin asked. "And you said her mom has a bodyguard looking after her."

"Yeah, but Sally can't be in two places at once if Kate finds a place of her own." Worry colored everything he saw and did. "The police can try to keep track of things, too, but..." His lips twisted. "It's not the same as having somebody with her every step."

Erin looked at Ranae who hunched into her shoulders. "Maybe one of us can get out there first..."

"No," Blake said harshly. "No. No one's going it alone anymore. Everyone needs to stay together for the sake of safety."

Ranae put a placating hand on his arm. "You said 'we're' before," she said quietly. "Does that mean you want us to go with you?"

"I think Kate will deal with me better if you are along, to act as a buffer," Blake said, not knowing how mad Kate might be still. "Plus, if you're all together and with me, no one needs to worry about anyone else." Another baffled swipe through his hair. "And we need to call Nichole. When'd she go home anyway?"

"Yesterday morning. I talked to her as soon as she landed and she's supposed to call tonight when she gets home from work," Erin said.

Blake nodded, looked at the wood paneled walls and the signs scattered around, he thought about how much Kate had loved this place. She'd loved the little Irish pictures and the Irish toasts and sayings. His gaze roved from the flashing sign that read *Killian's Red*, to the giant placard that advertised Guinness, to the tall open rafters in the ceiling. He glanced from table to table to see if there was anyone he knew, in part because Luke was never very far from his thoughts. If he could get his hands on the sonofabitch, it would be over and they could all stop worrying.

During the five days since Kate left, all he'd done was worry. He went from one thing he needed to do to another, wishing like hell that the moment where he could go after her would just *get* here already. Right now he was trying to pass the time as he waited for the waitress to bring the food he and the girls had ordered. He wasn't really hungry, but he needed to get away from the ranch, and he needed to talk to Erin and Ranae.

Mostly, he needed to go to Oregon as soon as possible.

"I think we'll leave the day after tomorrow." Blake leaned forward in his chair. That would leave his grandparents maybe a day without someone looking after things for them.

"Okay." Ranae nodded and took a drink of her iced tea. "I need to go in to work tomorrow for some orientation, but they don't want me to actually start for another three weeks. I can stay that long in Oregon."

"I'm not sure how long I can stay. But I'll just tell my boss I have to go." Erin smiled. "And since my boss is my mom, she has to let me."

"Good." Blake leaned back so the waitress could set their food down.

"Yeah." Erin stuffed a French fry into her mouth. "I'll tell Nichole tonight about the plans. She'll probably want to meet us there."

\*

"I have a job!" Kate laughed aloud as she shifted her car into neutral at the railroad crossing.

She couldn't believe how quickly things had come together since her arrival at her mother's. She'd found an adorable, furnished one bedroom house close to Maggie's. A brisk fifteen minute walk could get her there easily. The phone was hooked up, the satellite TV was installed and even the Internet worked. She'd have access to her friends again. Kate smiled as she waited for the red flashing light to turn to green. Two trains had already roared past, but the light was still blinking.

She shifted into first and let out the clutch when she saw the light turn green. The car sputtered ahead a few feet and died.

"Damn car," Kate said. "First thing I'm going to do when I get my first paycheck is get you fixed." She turned the key and smiled when the little engine rumbled to life.

After her interview with the principal of her new school, the drive home was a treat. She'd been too preoccupied before to notice the small winding road as it weaved its way into the tiny town of Rocky Fork, Oregon. The sun, just setting, painted the quaint white houses in a golden glow. A group of children played at the right hand side of the road. Older children on bicycles were giving the younger ones rides on the handlebars. She could hear their laughter even through the closed windows of her car. It gave her a twinge to see them so near the road, but the sun-washed afternoon seemed guarded against misfortune. No accidents would dare happen in such a light.

She followed the road as it meandered its way through the sleepy town, traveling back to Cottage Grove. A slim man in a waiter's apron swept the walk of a small family restaurant that had obviously turned into a place for the local loggers to grab a drink or two after the sun went down. As she drove northward, Kate could tell that the town had been grand in its heyday. She could see where the park had been built up and added to for the many children that were expected to come and play. Sadly though, they hadn't come to play nor had they ever seen the park. Their parents had never moved here. The paper mill where they were supposed to work, had been shut down. The town that was once booming now curled itself to sleep each night hoping for a better day tomorrow. A day that had a job for everyone. A day that heard the park fill with laughter.

At the end of a hidden side street stood a house that reached up to touch the sky. Kate suppressed the urge to stop and look with thoughts of going home and calling Ranae, Erin and Nichole. She wanted to tell them about her job and ask them if they'd received the gifts she'd sent.

Pulling into her long, narrow drive, Kate wasn't surprised to see Sally. Her mother's bodyguard came by every afternoon about the same time. She always had an excuse like, "cookies from your mom" or "Maggie just wanted me to run over and ask you to dinner." Kate smiled, wondering what tonight's excuse would be.

"Hey, Sally!" Kate called as she shut the door of her car.

"Hey, yourself." Sally grinned. "Maggie sent me over to see how your interview went."

Well at least the excuse is valid. "It went great," Kate said as she walked into the house. Knowing that Sally would follow, she left the door open.

"I still can't believe how fast everything worked out for you."

"I'm sure I had help." Kate winked at Sally. "I'm sure Mom knew I wouldn't stay with her so she scouted this out for me."

"How'd you know?"

"I've known her a long time." Kate grinned. "She knew just what I would want and she found it. Then pushed me in that direction."

"Does that make you mad?"

"Used to. I used to get really upset when she'd go around nudging me this way and that. But then I realized that she was just trying help me get what I really wanted even if I didn't know it yet."

"I know what you mean." Sally looked over Kate's bookshelf.

"Do you think she knows about you?"

"Being her bodyguard? No. But I think she suspects something. That's why she looked so hard to find a place for you close by." Sally's lips quirked sideways. "She wanted you close, of course, but she's got more than a bit of insight, too."

"I don't want her to worry." Kate frowned. "I'm fine. In fact you can tell her that I got a job, and that I'll be over tomorrow, she can fix me lunch and I'll tell her all about it. Or I can call her."

"No way. I don't want to go back empty handed. I'll tell her what you said, but you could call her and say you want strawberry shortcake for dessert tomorrow night. I love that." Sally smiled a toothy grin and flipped a book off the shelf. "Hey, can I borrow this? I haven't read it yet."

"Sure," Kate said, wondering if Sally was going to put some sort of surveillance device in it or if she was truly going to read it.

"See ya tomorrow." Sally waved. "And don't forget about the strawberries."

*

"Couldn't have picked a better spot," Luke said aloud as he settled on a fallen log. Surrounding him was a small grove of cottonwoods relaxing in the coming dusk. The old trees knew what to expect from a Colorado summer. Even though today was sunny and warm, the evening could be chilly. It could a beautiful morning, hot with the sun, but by afternoon a thunderstorm could roll over the mountains and turn the air to freezing. Just beyond the grove to the west was the river, flowing strong and muddy with run-off. That was a sure sign for those old trees. Real summer wasn't very far off so they continued to let their limbs grow and their leaves green.

Nestled across the road from the woods was a small, cozy house. Sitting pretty with its white fence, white trim and brightening windows from the setting sun, it waited for its new owner to come home.

He sat waiting for the same person. Pulling an apple from his pocket and a slate handled knife with silver flecks, he sliced the red skin, enjoying how the apple bled as the blade pushed through the flesh to the core. Making another slice, the piece was free to be eaten. He stabbed the blade deep into the piece, tilted the shining edge toward the sky and toasted, "I owe you a red rose." Then he smiled. His face was darker than before, his hair longer, but his smile was still the same. "This is a perfect place to get your attention, Kate."

He wanted to surprise her. When the time was right, he would wait for her again, too. She would bleed for him. Again. She would fight. Again. She would strike out with everything she had, but she would still fall beneath him with her red hair spread, blood seeping from her body. God, he loved thinking about it. About how her warmth would surround him as he raged and pounded into her. She would thrash and scream his name. Until she died staring up into his eyes. Staring forever, dreaming only of him.

Oh, yes he wanted it to be a surprise—for all of them. Tonight was just an attention getter.

And Kate would live, but someone would die. Luke was pretty pissed that he couldn't be there to see the death. "But I have to be patient," he gave himself a pep talk. "The house will blow, and that Ranae bitch will die. Kate will know I'm thinking of her. I won't get to see Kate's face. I won't get to see Ranae's face either, but I know what it will look like."

The explosion will be hot enough to burn her eyes together, sear her flesh to the bone. Her hair will be in tufts of black singe. Her face will look exactly like my mom and dad's faces the night I killed them. Luke nodded to himself, "Yes, I even know the smell."

Luke was transported back to that night. The night when he was twelve and supposed to be staying at a friend's house. But, that night he'd killed his father. He killed him because he beat his mother. He killed her because she was a dumb bitch and didn't fight back. He'd pleaded with her, screamed when his dad hit her, tried to fight him. She did nothing.

"She never loved me like I loved her," he moaned.

His mother's beautiful face swam before him. Bruises showed beneath the make-up. Sunglasses hid the pain. Anger in his heart raged until he saw another face. Kate's. Her laughter could be heard, her strength felt. Her eyes replaced his mother's. Kate's face—clear of bruising—filtered over his mother's until the faces were the same. Feeling a sudden cold, Luke pulled his jacket to his body and trembled with the tears until his eyes dried and then fell to a fitful sleep of his mother screaming, Kate screaming, him screaming.

Yes, Kate would live, but someone had to die.

Her roommate Ranae would do.

# CHAPTER 16

"I love my little house," Ranae sang as she pulled into the drive just as the sun was setting. "I think I'm going to get a dog or a cat or something to keep me company besides this darn paperwork I have to do." Ranae set her overflowing bag on the kitchen table and moved to open her mail. She saw several packages, including one with an illegible return address, but spying a small box with Kate's handwriting on it, she grabbed it first. She dug in a drawer for her sharpest knife, the one with a slate handle and silver flecks to cut the tape, but couldn't find it. So she tore at the tough cardboard and laughed out loud when she saw Kate's gift. *50 Gourmet Meals for One.* "Only Kate would see a book as the solution for anything." Ranae picked up the phone to call the number Kate had included on the inside of the book.

"Kate," Ranae said when her friend answered.

"Yes." Kate laughed. "I was just about to call you. Did you get my gift?"

"I just love the look of the recipe on page 25. It's Rabbit Stew for One." Ranae flipped through the book to laugh at another recipe. "How's the job hunting?"

"Really good. In fact I just got home from an interview. They hired me right there on the spot."

"Really? I mean of course they would. But wow. Really!"

Kate laughed. "Yeah, I get to teach summer school to seventh graders."

"God!"

"It'll be fun. I want to make it fun."

"Well, if anyone can make English fun for teenagers in the summertime, you can."

"Thanks. Speaking of teaching, how are things for you at school? Special Education and Counseling Director! That's wonderful."

"Great." Ranae still felt giddy at her title. "I'm just loving it. I technically don't start for another three weeks. Even then it will only be paperwork until the school year starts, but I've met some of my kids. We have a new student who's pretty messed up. He's really smart, but his home life is wrecked."

"I can't believe what parents can do to their children." It was something Kate never understood. "If I ever get to have my own kids, I'll do everything in my power to make sure they never wonder if I love them."

"This little boy sure wonders. He has a lot of love to give though. Seems to be always that way." Ranae shook her head. She knew exactly what that little boy did when he went home each day because she had done the same thing when she was a kid. She'd hidden and prayed she would be grown up soon so she didn't have to face the yelling and the fists in the living room.

"You're grown now and you create your own future."

"I know. I'm so excited. I love my little house. I'm going to plant flowers. Me, who never does anything with dirt, I am going to plant something."

Kate laughed imagining what Ranae would look like. "Make sure you get some of those cute garden gloves and a hat, a big floppy hat."

Ranae paused. She was stalling. She knew she had to tell Kate about the note she'd found, but didn't really want to because she sounded so happy. "Kate?"

"Yeah?" Kate laughed, but stopped when she heard the tone in Ranae's voice. "What happened?"

"I found a note."

"When?"

"The morning after you left. He knows you're gone. But I don't think he knows where.

"Why? What did it say?" Kate asked and berated herself for the pounding in her heart.

The words were etched in Ranae's mind. She didn't think she'd ever forget them. "It said, 'Where are you going, Kate? Don't worry, I'll find you!'"

Kate swallowed hard. "I wonder what he's planning to do."

"I don't know. But we're safe. Erin and I talk every couple of hours with each other and Nichole and with...Blake."

"Oh." Kate wasn't sure how she felt about that. The anger that had driven her across the country alone had dissipated somewhat. She was beginning to understand why Blake hadn't said anything to her about the other messages. "I feel bad about how mad I got at him."

"I figured you would."

"Well, why didn't you tell me or stop me from leaving?"

"Because nobody can *tell* you anything. You're stubborn," Ranae said in a stern, but loved-filled voice.

"Is that what you call it?" Kate smiled. "You know me."

"Yes, I do."

Kate paused. "How is he?"

Ranae thought about eating lunch with him and Erin yesterday. "He's pretty torn up. I've seen him a couple of times since the morning you left. He's miserable."

"I wish I could tell him I'm sorry in person, but...I start work in two days."

"You'll think of something."

"Summer school only lasts two weeks, I'll get paid and by then I should know if the school wants to hire me for the fall. So maybe I can come for a visit in between."

"Sounds great." Ranae wanted to tell Kate she'd see her in a few days, but knew Blake wanted it to be a surprise, a good one.

"Two weeks isn't so long," Kate whispered to herself after she hung up the phone.

*

Later, when her meal of macaroni and cheese and peas was finished, Ranae added beef and chicken to her shopping list. The days for college food were over and she needed to eat better since she could afford it. But still it was a perfect end to a great day. Having her own home was a wonder. Sometimes she still couldn't believe it. She danced around to the music from the stereo as she dusted and swept and put away her dishes from dinner. She even paused from time to time to look out the window and watch the clouds drift over the mountains. The wind was coming up and the sky getting dark. It would be a cold night.

She could have gladly watched the sky change and the first rain drops turn to a powerful summer storm, but decided instead that she needed to get serious about the pile of papers she'd brought home or she'd be up forever. She took a quick shower, turned up the heat and climbed into bed with her papers. It wasn't the wisest thing to do, turning the heat up for the night even though it was chilly because she'd probably be too hot by morning. But it was her house, her bill and her warmth. She didn't care.

Hours passed, but the thunderstorm didn't come. And in the dark hours of night her house settled around her while her purple pen made notes on the papers in front of her. Now they were welcoming, homey sounds, but when she'd first moved in, she'd made Kate stay up all night checking every noise. Now she knew them all and her heart no longer raced. Nevertheless, for the sake of "just in case," she kept her phone beside her bed. She knew that doing paperwork in bed was a bad habit and that she should be at the table in the kitchen, but she loved her bed. It was the first addition to her home. An old, tall wrought iron bed so heavy two people had to carry practically every piece. She could jump on it and it didn't creak. She knew because she'd tried it.

As she made her last note, Ranae yawned and stretched, getting ready to snuggle down into her comforter for the night. When she glanced over at her alarm to cringe at the time, she heard a loud pop. In an instant she was under her bed curled in a tight ball. She had no time to think it childish. No time to berate herself for not taking the phone with her. She had no time for her next breath.

Her house exploded around her.

*

The loud boom that echoed through the river valley awakened Luke. He sat up with a curse.

"How the hell did I fall asleep! Was the bitch even home?"

Luke peered through the haze and saw that yes, her car or what was left of it, was in the driveway. He laughed at the rich, red flames eating their way through Ranae's house as he walked away. The laugh stopped when he was almost a mile away. It turned to a scowl, when he heard the emergency vehicles' wails calling through the night.

"They're fast, but they won't find anything, except a pile of flesh and my nice little note for Kate," Luke said to himself as he walked the next half mile, started his car and cursed at the rain as it began to fall.

He had no idea that as he drove, firemen were already pulling the unconscious but alive Ranae from beneath her bed.

# CHAPTER 17

"How are you liking your little house, Dolly?" Maggie's happy voice called from the kitchen.

"Fine—great, I can't believe how fast everything is going. Are you sure you don't need some help?"

"No. That's why I sent Sally out to mow the lawn. That girl needs to keep her hands busy."

Kate nodded in agreement as she wandered from picture to picture hanging on the wall. Everything was here: the horses, the ranch, her at various rodeos, even the girls. "I still don't know how you hung up all of these," Kate yelled. The pictures were scattered over every inch of wall space. The mantle was covered, the shelves that were to be used for books even had pictures displayed.

"I had Sally help me." Maggie finished placing the cookies on a plate that she and Sally baked special for Kate's visit today. Kate knew Maggie was secretly pleased at being able to do little things for herself. Her mother wouldn't always be able to do them; a day would come when she'd have to depend on someone else for everything. But for now being able to count the steps to the refrigerator and get the milk and then count the steps to the cupboard and get the glasses and to be able to pour the milk was a blessing and she liked doing it by herself, for herself.

Kate stood in the doorway of her mother's tiny yellow kitchen and watched as Maggie poured the milk. Things were so different than they used to be. Years ago her mother could have filled two glasses in no time, but now she had to tip a finger over and inside the rim of the glass to feel when it was full. *My mama is so strong. I'm so proud at how she just keeps going,* Kate thought. When the glasses were full, Maggie felt for space as she placed the glasses on the serving tray next to the plate of cookies. Then she counted the steps back to the fridge, felt where to put the milk and set the pitcher in its place.

"Kate, do you want to carry this into the living room?" Maggie called.

Not wanting her mom to know that she had been standing in the doorway watching, Kate tiptoed to the outer edge of the living room and called, "Sure be right there."

Maggie smiled, hearing exactly what her daughter was doing.

"These taste just the same as they used to." Kate took a bite of her cookie as she settled into the overstuffed couch next to her mom.

"Sally follows directions pretty well. She used to say, 'Oh no, Maggie, we need a cookbook,' but now she trusts me and has even started writing down some of the recipes I keep up here." Maggie tapped her head.

"I think I need to write this one down." Kate grabbed another cookie. "I can't ever make my chocolate chip cookies taste like these." They were perfect cookies, chewy with just the right crisp, chocolate in every bite and a flavor that hers never had.

"Brown sugar and butter are the secret. No use making cookies if it isn't done right. Don't use any substitute butter and use only brown sugar," Maggie continued as she sipped her milk and nibbled her half cookie.

"I'll try that next time I bake them. How did I manage to grow up and not know how to make these?" Kate took a drink of the milk that her mom had delivered each day.

"I think you were too busy learning about other things."

Kate looked at her mother's face. Love shown through her eyes. The deep blue hadn't faded as the doctors said it might. Her eyes didn't wander independently either. When her mother faced Kate, it looked like Maggie could still see her.

Of course she could, Kate thought. "I'm sorry I didn't keep in touch as much as I should have," she said.

"What makes you think you should have?" Maggie questioned.

"I should have called more because you might've needed me."

"You needed time to figure out some things for yourself." Maggie leaned forward to search for Kate's hand. Kate reached back. "And I needed time to let you and to let myself learn that just because I couldn't ride horses and rope calves any more didn't mean that my mind wasn't strong. I needed to learn that I was still the same as before, but that my body wasn't."

Kate gripped her mother's hand. "How do you always seem to know what I am thinking? When I was a kid, I used to think you could see it, but I know that's not true, now. It couldn't be."

"Why isn't it true? Maybe it's a different sort of seeing." Maggie laughed. "Maybe it's that bit of Irish that was passed down from your grandpa." Maggie paused and thought a moment about her tall, beautiful daddy who could sing and dance with the best of them. He was such a dreamer. She could still see him, his red hair going gray standing at the edge of the Missouri River as it cut its way through the Nebraska landscape. "Bonny girl—t'isn't much like the Shannon, but it's ours isn't it? In that we have more magic than most any leprechaun." Then he'd wink his Irish green eyes like he was knowing something nobody else did. "But, more like it's the magic of being a mom. You'll know when you have your own." Maggie winked her deep blue eyes like she knew something no one else did.

"I hope so," Kate said.

"Of course it is." Maggie smiled wistfully. Then, as the timer dinged, she said briskly, "Well, you better go get Sally off that lawn mower and tell her lunch is ready. We're having baked chicken and it isn't good cold."

*

Back at the hospital in Colorado, Blake took a single look at Erin's tear-streaked face and swore. "Damn it. I have to call Kate."

"I called Nichole. She's waiting for us to tell her whether she should come here or if she should still meet us in Oregon."

"I don't know yet." Blake shook his head. "We'll see what the doctors say."

"I wish I'd been there when that son of a bitch was in her house. I would have—"

"Me, too." Blake started walking away. "I have to call Kate right *now*."

Behind him, Erin nodded and slumped into a plastic coated hospital chair. "I'll be right here."

Blake thought about calling from the lobby of the hospital, but decided privacy was more important than immediacy. Shutting the door on his truck he closed his eyes. This was the hardest phone call of his life. He punched the buttons of Maggie's phone number in Oregon. Because he talked to Sally every day, he knew Kate was there having lunch.

*

"I'll get it." In Oregon, Kate ran to the phone. "Be sure to save some of that strawberry shortcake for me." She laughed at Sally's big eyes as she looked at the whipped cream.

"No way," Sally yelled.

Kate picked up the receiver. "Hello, Maggie's White's residence."

"Kate."

"Blake?"

"Yeah, darlin', it's me. How you doing?"

"What's wrong?" Kate asked.

On his end, Blake shook his head. Of course Kate wasn't going to let him string it out. "Something's happened."

"What?"

"There was an explosion at Ranae's."

"Oh, God." Shock sent tears down Kate's cheeks.

"I'm sorry, darlin'. I wish I could be there with you."

"Blake, just tell me."

"It happened last night. She's alive, but hurt. I don't know how bad."

Kate squeezed her eyes shut. "I just talked to her last night. Is Erin okay?" She felt her mother's warm hand fold over hers.

"Yeah. She's swearing and crying, but she's okay. She's in the waiting room."

"Will you call me as soon as you know how bad she's hurt? I start work Monday, but I can maybe fly home for a day or two. And," she continued through Blake's protests, "don't tell me about Luke and what he might find out if I fly. If Ranae needs me I'm coming!"

Blake gripped the steering wheel as if that would give him the courage he needed for the next thing he had to tell Kate. "Darlin', listen. There's more. There was a letter. Luke sent it in a fireproof box. I guess he wanted to be sure the firemen would find it right away."

"What did it say?"

"It was to you."

Kate nodded even as her breath stuttered in her lungs.

"The first part talked about how he had rigged the furnace to explode. And that he planned on watching the house burn with Ranae in it." The letter had actually said, *with that Ranae bitch screaming*, but if Blake had any say in it, Kate would never see the letter. He didn't care what she had to say about it.

"Did he plan on Ranae dying? Never mind, of course he did. But he failed, didn't he?" Stupid idiot. "What else, you said the first part."

"The box looked like it had come in the mail, so the investigators aren't sure if Luke was even there or not."

"That's just a ploy. He's very smart. He was there, of course he was. But that's not what the next part of the letter said. Tell me what it said."

"It warned that none of the people you loved were safe and that neither were you. Luke said he would kill all of us."

"Did he mention names?"

"Yes." Blake drew a harsh breath. "Even Maggie's."

"Well, he won't succeed." The anger felt good, potent.

"Darlin', listen." Blake was beginning to worry that Kate wasn't taking Luke's threat as seriously as she should. Chief Barrs had faxed him a copy of the letter that morning. He'd tucked it away in the bottom drawer of his dresser. The words had scared him. "Across from Ranae's house the cops found a kitchen knife stuck in a stump. There were no fingerprints, but there was an apple core."

"That had to be him. He's probably thinking that he killed Ranae, that I am panicked and will let him get to me, too. Let him. He will think he has all of this power, but he doesn't. I'm not as stupid as he thinks I am." Rage practically bubbled from her pores. "Neither are my friends. Call me about Ranae." Kate hung up the phone and looked into her mother's eyes.

"Who's Luke and what did he do?" Maggie asked.

"Oh, Mama," Kate cried and leaned into her arms.

# CHAPTER 18

"Blake, the doctor said she's going to be fine. They were concerned with all the bruising, but the x-rays and all the other shit they did came back with no internal injuries." Erin smiled, relieved that her friend was going to be okay.

"When can she travel?" Blake asked. He wanted to make sure they made it to Oregon before Kate decided to come check on Ranae herself.

"I don't know. Her arm is broken, but they put a cast on it already."

"Can you find out? I need to go out to the ranch and ask Grandma if we can borrow her car. A truck's suspension would play hell on Ranae right now."

"Yes." Erin said as she watched Blake walk away again. He sure is good at that, she thought. I'm glad he's walking towards something now. Towards Kate is a good thing.

\*

"Why didn't you tell me all of this before?" Maggie asked after she heard the entire story of what had happened between Kate and Luke.

"I'm sorry I didn't. I didn't want you to worry more than I know you already worry." Kate wiped her eyes and shook her head. *I sound like Blake*, she thought.

"Well, now you have a chance to keep me involved." Maggie looked at Sally. "You, too."

"Yes, ma'am." Sally nodded.

"Are you really mad, Mama?"

"No. Not really. I'm sad that I thought I had a friend who was just a friend, but isn't. And I'm scared for you."

"Maggie, I am your friend." Sally sat on the couch beside Maggie. "It isn't just my job that makes me care for you. I truly do."

"That's good to know." Maggie reached for Sally's hand. "Now you get to tell me what you're doing to keep my little girl safe."

Relieved, Sally complied immediately. "For one, I talk to Blake every day to let him know how Kate is doing."

"What?" Kate asked.

"He said you'd say that." Sally smiled. "He also said to tell you that he would have called you himself every day to check on you, but that you needed time to be mad at him."

"Oh." Kate couldn't help smiling. *Maybe, I'm not so mad anymore*, she thought.

"Second," Sally continued. "I have surveillance equipment here and in Kate's yard and around her house. I'd like to get something inside her house, too, but thought I should ask permission."

"That sounds like a good idea," Maggie said.

Sally nodded. "I also keep in touch with the police in Colorado in case they learn anything before Blake does."

Kate looked up and glared at Sally. "Did you know about Ranae before Blake called me?"

"No. If I had, I would've told you."

"Good. Now tell me how we can catch Luke," Kate demanded.

"I don't know, Kate." Sally shook her head. "I wish I did. He's been on the run so long that he's really good at hiding and disguising himself. It'll take time."

"Or maybe somebody I love dying?" Kate eyes filled with tears again.

"I hope not," Sally said.

"Oh, Dolly. Me, too." Maggie wrapped her arms around Kate. "Me, too."

\*

"If you two don't stop fussing, I'm walking the rest of the way," Ranae grouched. Erin had tried to hand her a pillow for the last ten miles. Blake was just as bad with all the food he wanted to cram down her throat.

"What the hell's the matter with you? We're just trying to make you comfortable. But if you don't want our help, fine. I'll ignore your ass."

"Now listen, you two. We're almost there. Only about an hour more, if my directions are right. If you can hold off spitting at each other till then, that'd be great," Blake said for the hundredth time in the last day and a half. The only thing that changed was the length of time they had to wait to see Kate.

"Where do we pick up Nichole?" Ranae asked.

"He already told us. But I guess your highness was sleeping," Erin sassed.

Blake closed his eyes and asked for strength. "I'm supposed to call her when we're outside Cottage Grove. She's staying at a friend's condo in Eugene and will meet us at Kate's house. We're going to try to time it so we arrive at the same moment."

"That's really nice." Ranae said, dabbing at her eyes. Must be the pain medication they gave me, she thought. All of it was just so gosh darn *nice*. That included the big fluffy pillows Blake had bought for her to relax against. The whole new wardrobe of clothes he and Erin had picked out when nothing from her house was salvageable. Erin had picked out all new make-up for her, too. They had done everything for her so that all she had to do when it was time to go was step out of the wheelchair and into the car. "I'm sorry I am so cranky, you guys," she apologized now.

"Don't worry about it. We know it's just your broken appendage talking." Erin laughed.

Blake gave her a no-big-deal wink in the rear view mirror.

"We'll stop at the next gas station so you ladies can use the restroom, and I'll call Nichole to let her know we're close." Blake turned on his signal to take the next exit.

"Sounds good," Erin said as she watched Blake maneuver Leona's big Cadillac along the winding curves.

*

"Yes, Mama, I'm excited about tomorrow," Kate said into her phone.

"Do you want to come over for dinner? I think I've got some steaks in the fridge. We can celebrate your first day tonight."

"I think I just want to stay home. I'll have to get to bed early and if I'm here, I'm more likely to do that than if I'm over there with you and Sally."

"Yeah, I know we talk too much." Sally's voice carried through the receiver.

"Stop being a private investigator and get your own phone." Kate laughed and waved at the camera hidden in the hanging plant in her kitchen. She knew Sally was using an earpiece to listen to their conversation and could see her. Sally took a little security monitor everywhere with her. She decided doing that was easier than calling Kate all of the time. Being able to know what Kate was doing through Sally gave Maggie peace of mind because she could just ask, "Is Kate okay?" It also gave Kate a sense of privacy, even if it was pseudo-privacy.

"Well, maybe tomorrow night then. And you can bring your friends," Maggie said.

"What friends?" Kate asked.

"The ones pulling into your driveway right now." Maggie giggled. Sally had just told her that Blake was driving a long black Cadillac and Nichole was in her sporty red rented car.

"What?" Kate looked out her window and saw the cars pulling down the drive. When she heard her mother's laugh and Sally's good-bye she hung up the phone and raced to the door.

"Aaaah! O-My-Gosh!" cried Kate, laughter pouring from her

lips. "Hi! Ooooh! I'm so glad you came!" Kate moved to grab the girls one by one, but as always they moved into hold her and each other. "I've missed you so much." Kate stood and held them.

"We made it," Nichole said.

"Yeah. It took forever," Erin said.

"I'm glad you're here." Kate looked at Ranae. "I'm so sorry, Nae...I don't..."

"Don't even talk about it. I'm fine," Ranae said patting her cast. "A broken arm never hurt anybody. And besides, now you get to sign it."

"Okay." Kate searched Ranae's eyes. "How did you guys manage this?" She turned back to Nichole and Erin.

"We have been planning it for days. Actually, not we—Blake's been planning it," said Erin.

"Oh." Kate looked at Blake.

He was leaning on the fender of Leona's Cadillac, looking as handsome as ever, with his hat in his hand. She knew she had some apologizing to do. Especially now. So she walked to him, smiling.

Blake smiled back. He wasn't sure how this was going to go, but the smile was good. It was better than good. It was perfect.

"Hi, darlin'." Blake stepped forward and took her hand.

"Blake. I'm sorry for the way I—"

"Don't you dare apologize for a stupid thing I did. I should have told you. And before you say anything else, I want you to know that I don't think you're stupid or weak or helpless. In fact I think you're just the opposite of all of those. That's one of the reasons I didn't tell you. I knew you'd spend all your time taking care of us instead of taking care of yourself. And..." Blake paused. "I wanted to take care of you, for a change."

"I'm glad." Kate kept smiling and asked, "Are you hungry? I think I might have some food."

"Hell, yes. I'm starving," Erin hollered.

"Thanks, Blake," Kate said as she turned toward the house.

"For what, darlin'?" Blake smiled and linked his fingers with hers as they walked.

"For bringing them."

Blake brought her hand up to his lips. "You're welcome." He winked.

Kate felt his breath on her skin and caught her breath. She hadn't noticed that the warmth she felt inside when she was with Blake had been missing. She'd been too busy being mad at him. But now she felt it.

After dinner and more of their good natured arguments over where everyone was going to sleep, they settled down so Kate could rest. Blake sure thought of everything, Kate thought as she double checked her alarm clock beside her bed. He'd brought blankets, sleeping bags and a few extra pillows. The girls were lined up in her living room, probably still whispering and driving Blake crazy while he tried to sleep on the couch. At least that's what they were doing when she told them good night. The small living room was cluttered and filled in every corner. Extra blankets were piled along one edge. Suit cases lined the wall in various states of neatness. Smiling, Kate closed her eyes. She couldn't say for sure when she finally drifted off.

Blake couldn't sleep. He knew he should be able to. The girls had stopped chattering and he could hear their sleeping breathing, but his mind wouldn't relax. It kept replaying the afternoon. It was good to see Kate with her friends. Time or miles or even new kitchens couldn't keep them from laughing and teasing and working in the pace and flow of easy friendship. They finished each other's sentences and laughed before the joke was even told.

But that wasn't what was keeping Blake awake. It wasn't the small glances Kate threw his direction; those were certainly something to lose sleep over. Though the soft smile she'd sent him as she sliced cucumbers for the salad and the shining glint in her green eyes as she turned the grilling chicken was part of it.

No, what had him tossing on Kate's couch was something different. He had always known that Kate was the most important person in his life, apart from his grandparents. He loved her, always had. She'd been the constant in his life. But to find that he'd truly fallen *in love* with her today over barbequed chicken was a little bit of a surprise.

# CHAPTER 19

Kate awakened with a start. She shook her head, clearing it from the night's haze and looked at the clock that blinked four a.m.

"Might as well get up," she murmured and turned her thoughts to the day ahead of her. Today was her first day of school. She ate a quick breakfast, left a note for Blake and the girls and spent several minutes fussing with her hair and make-up. As she drove to the school in the still dark and misty world, Kate tried to push the dream she'd had from her mind.

It was a replay of the one she'd had since the explosion at Ranae's house. It was very simple. She was running along a wooded path and Luke was chasing her. In his hand he held a knife and screamed her name. But she never finished the dream. When she tripped over a branch in the path and fell with Luke looming above her, she woke up. That's what had pulled her from her sleep this morning.

As Kate sat at her desk, small rays of sunlight drifted through the mist and into the classroom. The dream was a distant thought as she went over her plans for the day.

"Good morning, Miss White," her principal's voice said.

"Good morning." Kate smiled and looked at Mr. Vincent standing in her doorway. He was wearing a gray suit and had a leather briefcase clutched in one hand.

"You're here really early."

"I wanted to make sure I had everything ready." Kate's voice rose with anticipation.

"Did your mother get to come up here and help you get settled into your room?"

"Oh, yes." Kate had mentioned Maggie in the interview. "She had a great time. Thank you for asking."

"You're welcome. I'm pleased that she had a nice time. Mrs.

O'Konel should be in soon so you can finally meet her since she was ill on the day of the interview. Two of her four children go to school in the elementary here. They're a wonderful family. I'm sure you'll get along fine." He smiled.

"I hope so. I'm sorry the room doesn't look exactly the way I'd like it to. I put together the bulletin boards and straightened as much as I could," Kate replied. "I'll work more this weekend."

Mr. Vincent stepped in for a better view. By his glance, he was pleasantly surprised to see what Kate had done with his old room. The bulletin boards were bright and neatly arranged with boarders and eye-catching phrases. The books that had been strewn about, were now shelved by size.

"It looks very tidy and professional." He nodded to the framed Oregon teaching license and college diploma hanging in the deep red-cherry frame behind her on the wall.

"Thanks." Relief visibly washed over her face.

"I'll check in at about ten."

"Okay," Kate whispered as she watched him walk away.

It was now almost seven. I have some time, Kate thought. She stood and walked around the room. She stopped at each bulletin board to double check them. The *The 8 Parts of Speech* and the *Poets of the World* boards did look nice. The gray-black burnt edges of the poetry pieces made the display seem interesting and mysterious. The bright red, white and yellow pieces made the nouns and verbs seem exciting and enticing. Just the way Kate wanted.

Continuing her final look through, Kate saw her name, "Miss White," written in her best handwriting on the chalkboard waiting to greet the students. The beanbags in the corner by the bookshelves were ready for the seventh graders' open minds. Excitement and fear filled Kate until she thought she couldn't take the waiting much longer.

"You look like you're either about to laugh or cry." A lilting voice with just a touch of Irish came through her open classroom door.

Startled, Kate looked toward the owner of the voice who stood in the doorway. Her arms were loaded with books. In one hand she held a set of keys, in the other a baby rattle and a water bottle.

"Hi, I'm Kate—White."

"I'm Coleen O'Konel." She smiled as she shuffled the keys to her other hand so she could shake hands with Kate. "Very nice to meet you. Mr. Vincent spoke very highly of you and I can see why by the looks of your room. You're a worker of magic."

"I'm glad to meet you. You're beautiful," Kate blurted. "I mean Mr. Vincent said you were Irish. Your name sort of gives it away."

Coleen laughed. "I am Irish, right you are, but so are you, my red haired lass. Thank you for the compliment. With the morning I've had, I sure needed it. How are things going?"

"Everything's fine. I worked pretty hard this weekend to arrange the room, put up posters and plan for the first couple of days, but I don't really know what the kids know. So I'll have to—" replied Kate.

"You'll do fine. I know I'm excited you're here. And I am right across the way if you need me."

"Thanks," chirped Kate. "Have a good day."

"You too. Oh, and by the way, you're beautiful too," Coleen added with a motherly pat to Kate's hand.

Smiling, Kate watched Coleen depart.

Time passed and the bell rang. Kate quickly hoped for the success of the day, gathered her papers and met her students at the door.

*

"It's so fun. The neatest thing is when I write something on the board, they write it in their notebooks," Kate said to everyone sitting at her mother's dinner table.

"Isn't that what they're supposed to do?" asked Erin as she filled her fork with mashed potatoes.

"Yes, but it's different when *you're* the teacher." Kate laughed.

"Well, I for one am glad you like it," Nichole said. "When Ranae said you were teaching English to seventh graders this summer, I thought you'd be miserable. I know I would."

"That's why I'm the teacher and you work in Hollywood. I would be miserable dealing with actors and writers and directors."

Nichole laughed at the thought of Kate working with all those people. She'd probably turn Hollywood on its ear though, just like Nichole hoped to.

"Is your principal nice?" Ranae asked.

"Yes. In fact he used to teach in the room that's mine now."

"So, Nichole, are we going to tell Kate our surprise?" Erin asked. "Because even though I really enjoyed listening to Ranae snore all night, I don't want to do it again."

"What," Ranae laughed. "I don't snore. It was Blake."

"Now, hang on a minute." Blake held up his hands. He'd been waiting for this to come up. He wanted to know what Kate thought about the idea. He, of course, was all for it.

"What's the surprise?" Maggie asked.

"I have a producer friend who lives in Eugene. I stayed at her condo when I was waiting for you guys to get here from Colorado. She only uses it every so often and she's not in town now. I asked her if Ranae and Erin could stay with me. That way we don't take up all the room in Kate's house."

"But—I don't mind," Kate said. "I like having you there."

"And we will be there, every evening. We just won't sleep there," Ranae said.

"Anyway, we think it would be good for *someone* to sleep there, so we nominated Blake. And it's not because he's a man. I'm not that damn sexist. It's because he likes your couch." Erin laughed.

Kate laughed, too, as did the others, but she still wasn't too sure about the arrangement. "Well—"

"Not to put a damper on the mood or anything, but I think for safety purposes, it's a great idea." Sally leaned forward and took a drink of her coffee. "I think we need to think about everyone being safe. I have a buddy who lives in Eugene who can set up some surveillance at the condo, so you girls will be taken care of. I can still be here with Maggie, and I know I would feel better if Blake was with Kate. He can be with her way more than I can."

"But don't you think—" Kate began.

"Dolly, I think that Sally's right," Maggie said. "We want *everyone* to be as safe as possible until the cops catch Luke."

"What do you think, Blake?" Kate asked.

"I want you to be safe, but I also want you to feel comfortable with whatever we decide to do. If you'd feel better, maybe Sally could stay with you and I could be here for Maggie." Blake took a drink of lemonade, hoping that Kate would let him stay with her. Getting up this morning and finding her gone with only a note was just about too much for him to handle. He wanted to be with her as much as possible.

"I guess it'll be okay." Kate took a bite of green beans. "I guess we need to do something until Luke is caught."

\*

Kate didn't want the girls to leave. Blake couldn't wait for them to go. He breathed a sigh of relief when he heard Erin say, "We'll go do that first thing this weekend" and then shut the door.

"It sounds like fun," Blake said from his seat on the edge of the couch.

"Yeah, we haven't shopped together for a long time. I think I might try to get something new. Something I've never—" Kate paused to look at Blake. "What's the matter?"

"Nothing." Blake couldn't stand it anymore. "Darlin'." He walked to her. "I…I'm—"

"What is it?"

Blake looked into Kate's eyes. He searched for fear or any sign that would tell him not to do what he so wanted to do. He saw nothing that would discourage him. But he hadn't done it yet.

He gently put his hands on Kate's shoulders and kept searching. His hands skimmed her arms and traveled to her waist. He pulled her body close to his and was glad when what he saw in her eyes had nothing to do with fear.

"Can I kiss you?"

Kate nodded.

Blake didn't wait. He lips met hers with all the urgency he felt. He felt like if he didn't hold her and touch her, he'd explode. He wrapped one arm around her waist. While his other hand made soft circles on her face and traveled through her hair, his lips explored. He made himself go slow. Made himself be patient.

Kate was lost in his kiss the second his lips touched hers. The heat from his tongue as it laced the edge of her mouth curled and shot through her body. Softening her mouth for him, she invited him to deepen the kiss. She pulled him in with her hands as they closed around his face.

He felt her surrender against him and he asked for more. He couldn't help himself. He needed her, loved her. The hand in her hair moved to her waist and he lifted her against him. Their bodies met in the perfect places. Falling slowly to his knees he wrapped Kate's legs around him and lay her gently on the floor. The kiss became more urgent. His hands begged for more as they moved up her body. He felt her arch as he filled his hands with her breasts. Need so strong it left him breathless as it slammed through his body.

Kate tightened her legs around him. She moaned against his touch. She wanted him. She wanted all he would offer. She could feel her tears on her cheeks as she moved her mouth with his.

"Blake, please," she murmured against his lips and pulled him to her with her hands.

Blake looked into her eyes. He was ready to do what her body was begging. But then he saw her tears. "Jesus, Kate. I'm sorry. Damn it." Blake stood and pulled Kate with him into his arms.

"Blake what are you—?" Kate couldn't understand the anger in Blake's eyes. She couldn't get her body to relax. She didn't want to. She felt wonderful and warm.

"Ssshh. Don't talk." Blake carried her to her room and laid her on her bed. Gathering a blanket from beneath her feet he spread it across her. "I'm sorry, Darlin'. I didn't mean to."

"Blake?"

"Just sleep, Darlin'," Blake said as he turned out the light and cursed himself. I should have known I couldn't just kiss her without taking it too far. Damn it. How could I have been so stupid, Blake thought to himself as he sat on the couch looking into the hours of another sleepless night.

# CHAPTER 20

The girls were there every night when Kate came home from work like they said they'd be. They'd eat dinner, laugh and chat until Kate had to go to bed. And Blake would scowl or be candy cane sweet.

It was driving Kate crazy.

She'd tried to talk to him about it, but he just said nothing was the matter and wouldn't say another word. So she figured going shopping with the girls would be fun.

"Blake, are you sure you don't care if I go shopping with the girls?" Kate asked trying to get a rise or something out of Blake.

"No. I don't care. But will you take my cell phone so you can call if you need anything?"

"Yes," Kate said as she picked up the phone. "Do you want to come?"

"No." Blake didn't even look up from reading the newspaper. He had no idea what it said. It could have been written in French and he wouldn't have known. He was glad a new one came every day because when Kate left for work, it was a joy to rip it to shreds and throw it away. He'd been dreading the weekend, knowing that Kate would be home for two days straight and that he'd have to deal with her, smell her scent, hear her laugh. He was going mad or maybe he was already there. He didn't know.

"Okay. Well, bye. Be back soon." Kate looked at him. His head was bent over the paper in his hand. His behavior confused her. She didn't know what she'd done wrong or even if she'd had done anything at all. *I'll find out tonight*, Kate thought as she got into the car with Erin, Nichole and Ranae.

"So tell me again what we're doing," Nichole said as she pulled out of the drive.

"We're going shopping for silly shit," replied Erin.

"Like what?" Nichole asked in a wary voice.

"Edible underwear," Erin laughed.

Nichole made a horrible face.

"The deal is this. You have to find the goofiest, silliest thing to buy. We buy butt loads of it. Then we come back here and use it all." Erin rolled her excited eyes at Ranae.

"I don't really know about this," Nichole said still not convinced.

"Oh. Come on, it's fun," Ranae encouraged. "One time Kate and I found these crazy leopard skin pantyhose. They were so outrageous. We wore them to a '70s party. It was great!"

"Yeah, and nobody really sees you anyway," Erin insisted. "I had purple eyebrows once. I wonder if I can have orange or green this time," she said more to herself than anyone.

"Really. We don't know anyone here. You're in Oregon, not California. You won't see these people again. Besides, we don't get anything that's permanent," Kate added.

"Okay," Nichole agreed.

"Damn straight. Glow in the dark toe nail polish for her!" Erin raved.

Nichole just rolled her eyes. The girls chattered non-stop all the way the shops. Kate, however, was mostly silent, but she did laugh when Ranae had Erin fired up over hair clips not being silly enough—even though they required batteries and played songs.

"Let's go into that shop that has the edible underwear first," Erin said as they got out of the car and howled as she saw the stricken look on Nichole's face.

"What?" Nichole screeched. "I'm not—"

"You are too. You said you would. Sheeesh. You'd think out of all of us you would be the most adept at this kind of thing. We live in the damn sticks after all—you live in L.A.," Erin argued.

"Fine. Fine. But I am not buying any flavored underwear." Nichole decided.

"If you're going to be a chicken shit about it, I'll get you some myself. Cherry is really good!" Erin giggled all the way to the store's entrance.

"The NOT-y Store" flashed neon in the shop's window. Walking between the long ropes of glittering beads that covered the entrance, the girls laughed at the small bright signs posted along the walls.

"Your mother's NOT here." Erin pointed and laughed at the sign.

"I like this one." Ranae motioned toward one that read: *If you're NOT 21 don't even bother.*

Nichole laughed. "It's like Halloween all the time."

Wigs, fingernails, lipstick and goofy lotions were there by the bag full. Erin of course went straight for the body paint. Ranae went to see about eyelashes and flashy nail polish. Kate wasn't particularly interested in anything really, but decided she wouldn't mind finding a feather boa. That might be fun.

Meanwhile, Nichole was trying to disappear into the corner near the stuffed people who were supposed to look like famous stars. There was everything from Sponge Bob Square Pants to Cartman from *South Park*.

"Erin loves this kind of stuff. She won't take no for an answer. But try to get her to do something she doesn't want to do and, well you know how she is," Kate said trying to set Nichole at ease.

"I know. I just like giving her grief. She's nuts." Nichole reached up and pulled down a little guy with a red sweatshirt. "Hey, this is Kenny from *South Park*. Remember, when we would have *South Park*-a-thons?"

"Yeah, that show was a real craze. I wonder if anyone on campus still eats popcorn and stays up all night watching it." Kate replied.

"Who was Erin's friend who used to sound just like Cartman?" Nichole asked.

"God, who knows. But he was really funny."

"Do you think me buying Kenny is silly enough for Erin?"

"I'm sure she'll be over any minute to grill you about what you're buying. Save it and we'll ask her," Kate added.

"Yeah." Nichole paused. "What's the matter, Kate?"

"Nothing. Why?"

"Because you seem sad. I just wanted to know if you're okay."

"I guess I am," Kate said and smiled as Ranae and Erin walked up. "I just don't know what to do about Blake."

"Why? What happened?" Erin asked as she smelled a bottle of massage oil.

"The other night after you guys left, he kissed me."

"Well, that's good right?" Ranae asked.

"I mean *really* kissed me. Not a peck on the cheek kind of thing. And I think I upset him."

"What do you mean?" Nichole wrapped her arms around her Kenny doll.

"I was crying."

"What the hell? Why? Did he hurt you?" Erin practically shouted.

"No. No." Kate smiled. "He didn't hurt me. I was crying because I felt normal. Not scared at all. I tried to talk to him about it, but he won't discuss it with me."

"Do you think he's mad?" Ranae picked up an incense wand, smelled it and put it back.

"About what? That's the thing. I don't know. I hope not."

"I know what you need to do." Erin smiled.

"What?" The girls asked all looking at Erin.

"You guys just need to strip down and have some hot damn sex," Erin said.

"I don't really think that's going to solve our problem." Kate picked up a keychain that read, *My Other Car Is a Rolls.*

"Why not? Sounds like you guys just need to get back in the saddle." Erin wiggled her fingers in the air.

"Kinda difficult for us to get back in a saddle we've never been *in*," Kate replied.

"What the hell are you talking about? Are you telling me you and Blake have never *ever* had sex?"

"You don't have to yell. I'm sure the people in this store don't care about my sex life. And yes. That's what I am saying." Kate's lips twitched. She knew Erin was about to croak.

"How come I never knew that? I thought you had." Erin jammed her finger a Kate.

"I knew," Ranae stated.

Erin's face looked as if she had just been sabotaged. Her gaze raced to Nichole.

"*I* didn't know," Nichole said as fast as she could manage. But Nichole did know. She'd been involved in the should-I-have-sex-with-Blake discussion years ago.

"Oh. Well, I guess it pays to be a roommate," Erin sassed. "But why the hell haven't you?"

"Rodeo was always more important."

"Well there's no rodeo now, is there?" Erin pointed out.

"No, there isn't." Kate looked at her tennis shoe covered feet.

"Ah, hell, Kate I didn't mean that. I'm sorry." Erin grabbed a hold of Kate's hand. "I just meant that there's no reason now why you shouldn't have sex with Blake."

"I know." Kate squeezed Erin's hand. "I'll think about it."

"Good." Erin sounded like she felt like a jerk about the whole conversation.

Kate didn't want Erin to feel terrible. She herself wasn't feeling bad, exactly. She just didn't know what to do where Blake was concerned. Having sex might not be that bad of an idea. He was the only one she'd ever wanted anyway. If talking to Blake later that evening didn't work, maybe she'd try the sex idea.

"We should get back to shopping," Ranae said. "It looks like Nichole has one of her choices."

"Hmmm," Erin said eyeing Kenny.

"Is this silly enough to meet the silly shopping standards?" Nichole asked.

"No, but if you really want it, I'll buy you some cool ass, hot pink hair jelly to make up for it."

"No," Nichole replied as she stuffed the Kenny doll back onto the shelf. "I guess I'll find something else. I really don't want hot pink hair."

"Chicken!" Erin turned to Kate and said, "Now let's get to shopping before all the good silly shit's gone. We have to get eye glitter next." She trotted off down another aisle smelling and testing as she went.

"Well, I guess we had better get going," Kate said.

"You know, I think I'll get some of those edible undies for my sister. Grape's her favorite flavor." Nichole giggled.

By the time the girls got back to the car after shopping and eating lunch, they'd argued and traded and traded back their silly shopping loot. Along with her feather boa, Kate bought some fake eyelashes. She always did. Her own were practically nonexistent. Besides she liked to pretend she was Elizabeth Taylor.

Pretty quick the girls were trying out their toe polish, nail art, glitter pens, long dangling earrings and a tinted face cream. It soon cluttered every inch Nichole's backseat.

"You guys be careful with that. This is a rental." Nichole looked in the rearview mirror with a worried face.

"I can't wear that. It'll turn my hair green," Ranae yelled as Erin tried to smear hair jelly into her hair.

"Well the damn stuff won't show up on my brown hair—so we have to try it."

"Absolutely no way!" Ranae pushed Erin out of the way.

"Chicken ass. I'll ask Nichole," Erin said as she got out of the car at Kate's place.

"No," Nichole said even before Erin asked and shut the door on her car.

Erin turned to Kate. Kate could feel her examining the color of her hair as they walked up the sidewalk. But before Erin could ask, Kate saw it.

Lying beautiful and deadly against the green moss on the stone walk was a long stemmed red rose. The sight of it brought back that night in a flash. She could feel the thorns tearing her skin. She could hear Luke's evil voice as he promised his worst. She could smell the sweet rose turn rotten with his breath. She could see the petals drift from his fingers like blood dripping from her veins.

As if in a trance, Kate picked up the note beside the rose and read the message. *I have found you, you bitch. Did you really think you could hide from me? Our time is close. And then your friends will soon join you.* Kate heard his rasping voice say the words, felt the memory of all the pain and then slipped silently to the ground.

She didn't feel the three girls try to catch her. She didn't hear their screams for Blake or his swearing as he raced up the walk with Sally and the police.

# CHAPTER 21

"I didn't really mean for you to see it, darlin'," Blake said as he tucked a strand of Kate's hair behind her ear. "I was definitely going to tell you about it, but I didn't want you to really see it. We left it there for the police to get evidence and pictures and stuff." Blake berated himself for his stupidity. He'd been wandering around Kate's house feeling sorry for himself, when he got a call from Sally saying that there was some activity outside the door. By the time he got outside, there was no one to be seen. He didn't even read the note before he took off in the direction Sally said the guy went. But he didn't find anyone. There weren't even any tracks to be certain about.

"That's okay," Kate said as she sipped her water. "I just can't believe I passed out."

Blake knew his heart would never beat the same. Seeing Kate lying limp on the ground was more than it could take. "I can. You've been overloaded with school and entertaining the girls... and me...maybe we shouldn't have come."

"What do you mean? Of course you should have. Besides I love teaching. Having you and the girls here is not an overload. And I enjoy entertaining you. I'll just be sad when you have to go back." Kate set her water on her nightstand.

"The girls can't stay very much longer, but I'm not going back." Blake sat on the edge of Kate's bed.

"Not going back? Why not? Leona and Jack can't run the ranch without you." Kate looked up, surprised.

"Casey Hilton is running things."

"Casey? Really." Kate could remember little Casey running after Blake like a puppy wanting to do everything Blake did. Time really flies I guess, she thought. "But you can go back, you know."

"No I can't. I can't go, because I won't. I'm staying here with you."

"Why?"

*Because I love you*, Blake wanted to say, but knew it was probably too soon to say it. He didn't want Kate to feel like she had to say it back. "Because I need to be here with you. I want to be here in case you need me."

*

Kate couldn't believe what she was hearing. She had never known Blake to put anything before the ranch. She'd always understood that, especially when the ranch was a family tradition, a way of life and livelihood. She'd often dreamed of being part of it. But to hear him say he wasn't going back and that he was staying with her was wonderful. Maybe he was beginning to love her as she had loved him all these years.

"How long are you going to stay?" Kate asked with a happy heart.

"As long as it takes."

"As long as what takes?" Kate smiled.

"Till he's caught."

"Oh." Kate looked at the comforter wrapped around her and felt suddenly cold. He was only here for Luke. Of course he was. He felt responsible. Decent men took care of their responsibilities. *Too bad,* Kate thought. She tried to shake off regret. "How long was I asleep?"

"Not long, in fact if you feel like it, Sally has a video recording of the guy who left the rose, do you want to see it?" Blake asked and wondered why Kate looked suddenly sad.

"Yeah. I feel like it. Let's see if it's him." *Let's catch him so you can go home*, Kate thought.

Kate watched in silence as the figure dressed in hippie-like clothes strolled up to her porch, set the rose down, and walked away. She couldn't see his face, but she didn't have to. It wasn't

Luke. Luke was taller and wider than the almost boy he'd had deliver the message.

"It's not him," Kate said.

"How do you know?" Sally asked.

"I know." Kate looked at her.

"I don't think it's him, either," Ranae said.

"Me either." Nichole patted Kate's hand.

"That guy's too scrawny." Erin pointed to the television.

"Well, gentlemen, that's it then," Sally said to the police standing behind the couch. "Thanks for coming. I'll be in touch." Sally nodded and waited for them to tip their hats and leave. "Now, what?" She asked the girls and Blake.

"I think one of us should be with Kate all of the time," Nichole said.

"Yeah. That's great. We can get killed, too." Erin stood up. "No. I'm sick of this shit. Why can't they find him? Why can't they go get that kid who was on the television and make him tell them where this son of a bitch is?"

"I don't know. He's really good for one," Sally said in a calm voice. "For two I think Kate confuses him."

"Now, you're a criminal psychologist?" Erin asked.

"I have a degree in it, yeah. But that's not what I'm using as my base here. I've studied the other cases, the other girls. Kate's the only one who fought back. I mean really fought back, which is something his mom never did. I guess his father used her as his punching bag. At least that's what the police reports say. Anyway, I think he admires Kate as much as he wants or needs to kill her."

"That's a hell of a thing to say with Kate sitting right here." Erin pointed to Kate.

"No, she's right." Kate stood and walked to Sally. "So what do I do?"

"If you really want to catch him, you're going to have to let him come to you?"

\*

"No, ma'am." Blake stood up, fear gripping his heart. He could hardly breathe. "We will think of something else. I will not let this happen."

"I think it'll work," Kate said.

"It's how my mom killed him," Ranae said. Tears were streaming down her face.

"Nae, no." Kate wrapped her arms around her friend. "Don't think about it."

"But it might help you." Ranae wiped the tears from her eyes. "My…attacker is dead. I don't have to be afraid of him anymore."

"But you are," Nichole whispered and joined arms with Kate.

"See what you did." Erin glared at Sally as she went to be with her friends.

"No. I want to tell it." Ranae sniffed. "You guys just hold onto me though, while I do."

The girls nodded and didn't let go.

"My mom was really young when she met my dad. He was this wonderful son of a rich family. But after they died, he started gambling to ease his grief, I guess. He lost all the money and began blaming it on my mom. See, his parents died on the way to their wedding. The way he saw it was, that if he hadn't been marrying my mother, his parents wouldn't have died. So, no matter how hard my mom worked, it was never enough. So he," Ranae paused and let the fresh tears stream down her cheeks, "beat her." She clenched her eyes shut and tried to ignore the vision of fists hitting bone.

"I can finish, Nae," Kate said. "Let me finish."

Ranae nodded.

"Nae's mom worked out this plan to get rid of her husband. All she really wanted was for him to leave her, but he never would. Always spouting the, 'til death do us part.' So, basically, she decided to kill him. She left this big elaborate note for him to meet her at this old plant, where to go when he got there and what to do. All under the assumption that she'd found a way for it to make money. In her note she told him how to turn the lights on. But what he was really doing was turning the boiler to an unsafe level. It all had to be timed just right. As he turned the knob, the lights had to come on."

"That was my job," Ranae said. "I remember being so scared. But I did it. Mom and I were back home by the time we heard the fire truck sirens. I can still hear her say, "God, please let him be dead. Please let him be dead." I think she would've died if he hadn't been."

"Dear God, Ranae." Blake hugged her close. "I didn't know. I'm sorry." No wonder she got under her bed so quickly, he thought.

"So how can we trick Luke?" Nichole asked, still not convinced this was a good idea.

"I'd like to have a few hours to do some thinking. I've thought of a few ideas, but I want to get them cemented in my mind before I involve you," Sally said. "In the meantime I want you to remember, you are all important to me. And that I gave Maggie my word that I would protect you. And I will." She turned to go, thinking of her own mother, the only person she'd ever failed to protect. "It's funny and awful how the world is the same," she muttered as she started her car. "But there's only so much a ten-year-old girl can do for her mom. This time I won't fail."

After Sally had gone, Kate hugged Ranae. "I'm sorry the shopping trip got ruined."

"No big deal." Nichole walked to look out the window.

"Nichole's a chicken ass anyway," Erin said, joining Nichole.

"Yeah, that's the breaks," Ranae said.

Blake sat down and scrubbed his hands over his face. *What the hell am I going to do now?* he wondered.

Kate looked at them. She loved them all so much. If luring Luke into a trap would save their lives and possibly hers, then she would do it. But she wanted to wait until summer school was over, only one more week. She'd tell Sally first thing in the morning. Right now, though she was going to bed.

"Hey, guys, I'm exhausted. I'm going to bed," Kate said and hugged each girl. "Good night, Blake." She kissed him gently on the head and walked to her room.

"What do you think, Blake?" Nichole asked.

"I think it's a horrible idea. But I know Kate will do it, especially if it means saving our lives."

"Can't *you* tell her not to?" Erin pointed at him.

"I wish I could. But I'm not going to. The last time I did something like that—" *I almost lost her for good*, he thought.

"Even if it means saving her life?" Nichole wiped a tear from her cheek.

"I don't know," Blake said. "Damn, I wish Sally would've never brought that up."

"We can't go on like this forever, you know," Ranae said. "It may work for a little while, but don't you think us trapping him is better than him trapping us? I do."

"I'd like to just kill him myself." Blake stomped to the kitchen.

"It's going to be Kate's fight." Ranae walked over to Nichole and Erin. "It always has been. Just like it was my mom's fight. But that doesn't mean we can't turn on the lights when the time comes."

"Damn right," Erin said and wiped tears of her own.

"Let's go plan how to get rid of Luke then." Nichole opened the door. "Blake, we're going," she called as the girls walked out in front of her. She understood him, understood his fear. She could see in his eyes how much he loved Kate. Nichole just wished he'd tell her soon. That love would give her strength.

Behind them, Blake waved a silent good-bye and felt like slamming the glass he held in his hand across the kitchen. In fact he'd love to see it shatter in a wild tide of shards. But he held firm. He was a Spencer.

He needed to pull himself together. Kate needed him and he was not going to let her down this time. But by God, if he ever got a hold of Luke he would gladly strangle the life from him.

*

Kate slept easy that night. She was snuggled down in her wide bed with the soft comforter tucked beneath her chin. She was dreaming. She was strolling along a winding path through the forest. In her hand were fragrant wild blossoms. She could hear humming and knew it was her own voice. The sun shone in little droplets of light on the fallen leaves at her feet. In the brush ahead of her she could see a tiny fawn hidden from the world by the wonder of its coat. She'd been walking for hours, loving every step. But for some reason she felt hurried. Like if she looked behind her she'd see someone she was afraid of. She couldn't think of who it would be. But then she heard him.

*Kate,* came the rancid whisper. *Kate, I'm following you.*

Kate started to run. She could hear his pounding steps matching her own. She looked over her shoulder and there he was. His knife glinted sliver as he ran.

*Don't run, Kate. I need you.*

She turned to see how close he was. He was there. A breath away. She begged her legs to run faster. Her blood was pumping fast. It throbbed through her aching muscles. She ran. Following the bend in the path she raced. But her foot got caught. She fell. She tried to scramble over the branch and get up, but he was there, looming over her.

Kate tore at the sheets in her bed. She woke up, but she couldn't drag herself from the dream. She was trapped. She was trapped with Luke standing above her.

*Why were you running, Kate. Don't you want me anymore? I want you.* Luke knelt over her, pinning her to the dirt. He slathered his tongue along her face. She could feel his hot breath. He held the knife high over his head, screaming, *Dream of me, you bitch! Dream of me, now!*

Then he slammed the blade deep into her heart. Over and over he stabbed. Kate could feel the life flowing out of her. She screamed.

# CHAPTER 22

Blake was tired. Night after night of no sleep was catching up to him. He didn't think he'd ever been this tired. Not even during his rodeo days, when traveling for three days straight to get to a rodeo where a bucking horse would throw him to the dirt, was common. He felt like it was at least two in the morning even though the clock on the mantle said it was still early.

He closed his eyes, wishing his mind would relax into the calming silence of the night. Feeling himself drift, he smiled. He swayed at that edge between sleep and awake. He was falling closer and closer to sleep's oblivion—until he heard her scream. Kate's piercing scream filled the house with terror. In an instant Blake was in her room.

"Kate, wake up." Blake was standing at the edge of Kate's bed. He practically pulled her to a standing position. "Come on, wake up." He was terrified at the panic on Kate's face. "It's not real. I'm real. I'm right here. Come on." Blake knew he was yelling. He had to, to be heard above her screams. When he saw her eyes flutter open, he quit yelling. "That's right. It's not real." Blake pulled her to him. "I'm real." He crushed her mouth with his. "I'm real. You're all right, darlin'."

"Blake?" Kate asked in a hoarse whisper.

"I'm here. Sshh. I'm here." Blake looked at her simple but sexy white cotton gown. His heart tugged at him.

"He killed me, Blake."

"Damn it, no, he didn't. You're right here. I'm holding you." He kissed her with all the passion he had in him. "I'm kissing you. Damn it! Do you hear me?"

"Do it again," Kate whispered.

"What?"

"Kiss me. Kiss me again, Blake. It makes me feel normal."

"You are normal."

"Just kiss me," Kate begged.

He was on the bed in a second, with Kate molded beneath him. His mouth ate at hers. Devoured hers. He moaned with need as she did. He pressed where she arched. He could feel her tears beneath his hands, but they didn't stop him this time. He needed her with his very soul. Life wasn't worth living without her. There would be no breath he'd take if she didn't share it with him. He moved his mouth from her lips to her cheek. Her scent engulfed him. His lips traveled the delicate line of her jaw down to her neck. Pulling the edge of her gown off her shoulder, he explored the curve of it. He knew he never be full of her. He'd never be done.

She twined her legs with his.

"Blake, please." Kate gripped his hair in her hand.

"Are you certain?" Blake paused and wished with all his might he'd still be able to function if she said no. "We don't have to do this."

"I want to." Kate pressed her lips to his and teased them with her tongue.

"I need to know." Blake flipped on the dim light on the bed stand. "I need to see you."

Tears edged Kate's eyes. "I'm sure, Blake."

Blake looked deep into Kate's eyes. All he saw was need that matched his own and something else, something else that had always been there. He just hadn't realize until now what it was. He'd had to love her first in order to understand that the something else that was always there was love. She loved him, just as he loved her.

Keeping his eyes locked on hers, he kissed her deep. Watched for fear. Fire flamed. The kiss turned hard and grasping. Kate returned it.

"Blake, please."

Blake wasn't sure if his voice would work. He nodded and nudged his mouth against hers. "You're not afraid?"

"Yes. I am."

Blake's eyes gazed into hers. He was certain he saw no fear.

"I'm afraid you'll stop. Again. I don't want you to."

"Darlin', I won't. Just give me a minute, okay? I want this to be special."

"Blake, it is special—"

"Sshh." Blake kissed her, switched out the light and left the room. A few moments later he returned with matches to light the candles that were set about Kate's room. After lighting one, he kissed her. On the lips. He lit another, then kissed her neck, her hand. He kissed her until all the candles were burning and he heard that sound of surrender every man waits for. With Kate, it was a sound so powerful and sweet. Blake ordered his pulse to slow.

Slipping beneath the covers and reaching for her, he found her warm and waiting with nothing between them.

"Oh, God, darlin'."

Threading her fingers through his hair she pulled him to her. Onto her. His mouth met hers. Sweet floating warmth worked its magic through her body. She pushed her body up to meet his. Surrendering, she turned her head as he kissed her throat.

He could see her heart beat through her skin. He paused only a moment to see what his hands could do to it. His fingers teased and coaxed her body until he felt he could conduct the orchestra of her pulse. Moving, slowly down, he cupped her breast. It swelled and filled his hand as his thumb drew loving circles, drawing it tighter with each pass. He replaced his thumb with his tongue. Taking her inside his mouth was a wonder. He felt her tighten against his tongue. He moved to the other to feel its response. He tightened as she did.

She grabbed his shirt, dragging it over his head. Skin on skin, heartbeat with heartbeat, she arched against him and pleaded with her hands. Her lips hummed along his shoulder urging him on. Her hands moved like a whisper of a breeze along his skin. Her fingers smoothed the muscle of his stomach. She smiled as it bunched with her movement. Following the tense muscles lower to the drawstring of his pants, she unlaced them. She pushed them down and away, running her tongue on his skin as she went. She kissed and teased and gathered him in her hands.

In a flash, he had her hands pinned above her head. "Darlin, just wait." His eyes smiled with promise. He reached over to the nightstand and unwrapped the condom he'd gotten from his duffle along with the matches. He strained against his need when her hands helped him put it on.

He smoothed his hands along her back, along her waist. Rolling with her. Moving her beneath him. He pulled her legs up around him, pressed his hips to hers. He smiled at the throaty moan escaping her lips. Slowing the rhythm, he kissed her lips. Trailing lower, starting over. Making it last. He wanted to enjoy her silky skin, her fiery hair.

He filled his mouth with her. He found a little spot at her hip that made her giggle when he skimmed it with his hands, but made her groan and arch toward him when he kissed it. He experimented with the other side to find the same. As his fingers found her wet and ready, he looked into her eyes as they moved. Slipping his hand over her, he saw her eyes grow dark and wide. This was something they'd never done and he wanted to watch her take that tumble. He wanted to feel what he could do to her. Wrapping his arm around her, he held her while his fingers found the spot he searched for. Soft and easy he moved.

He smiled into her eyes as she moved beneath his hand. He could see she was almost there. He gently moved faster and faster, pulling and begging her to trust him to care for her as she rose to the highest peak and then drifted back again. He felt her tense as she flew. He rocked her and kissed her back to earth and then moved above her to kiss her again.

"I want you, Blake." She arched against him. Pulled at him with her legs. Begged with her eyes. "I want you inside me."

She was all he saw. All there was. "Kate, I love you." He slowly slid into her. Warmth and need enveloped him. He wanted to drive deep and hard, but he felt it. He felt the tightness that said she'd never been with a man. He froze. "God, Kate, I didn't know."

"Of course you knew. I waited for you." Binding her legs tighter she pulled him in, deeper into her, wrapping herself around him. She opened for him. "I waited for this." There was no pain. Only need and urgency.

His vision blurred, his blood raced. He moved. That dive over the edge. They trembled with it. They rode with it. Rhythm with speed, with grace they moved toward sharp release. Wave after wave of tingling passion built and built until shattering between them, in them. Holding her breath, Kate willed the feeling to last forever. The waves smoothed out to ripples and the ripples to calm.

"Open your eyes, darlin', so I can see you."

Heavy lids lifted. Kate's green eyes held lingering warmth.

"I'm glad you waited."

"Mmmhm." Kate snuggled in deep beneath Blake.

"I remember meeting this fun loving, beautiful girl who rode a fast horse in a cow town in Colorado." Blake smiled and combed her hair with his fingers. "She was a wonder on the back of that animal. I'll never forget her red hair flowing out behind her in the setting sun of the evening. I fell in love with her at that instant."

"You did?" Kate whispered.

"Oh, yeah. I probably would have loved you my whole life and never talked to you if you hadn't been getting your check from the rodeo secretary at the same time I was. It took all the nerve I had to ask you to dinner."

"How come you waited so long to tell me?"

"I only figured it out a few days ago." Blake smiled.

"Well, I fell in love with a cowboy that night too. You looked so brave and scared and beautiful on that back of that buckskin."

"Beautiful?" Blake tickled her into a giggle.

*

"Yes, beautiful." Kate remembered that night so well. It was her favorite memory of Blake. The Blake she met on that night long ago was tall and skinny with ruddy hair that fit his deep blue eyes shadowed by long lashes that shouldn't have belonged to a boy. He smelled of the earth and horses and a new pair of Wranglers. He had drawn a rank horse for the rodeo that night and didn't even blink. After the rodeo, he convinced her that they should eat dinner. He called her beautiful. Her sixteen-year-old heart melted.

"I missed you so much." Tears streamed down her cheeks. "Why'd you go? I needed you."

"Darlin', I'm sorry. I can't tell you how sorry I am. I was weak and stupid." Blake held her against him and kissed her until her tears stopped. "But I'm here now. I love you. I'm not leaving."

"I love you too, Blake," Kate whispered as her eyes fluttered closed.

*

Blake was beyond exhaustion, but the magnitude of what had just happened kept him awake. He held Kate in his arms, wanted to until morning. He wasn't sure if he'd be able to sleep again. The need for Kate hovered at the edge of his senses, but fear gulped and tore at his heart. The fear of what could've happened with Luke. What if he had succeeded? What if Kate's first—and only— time had been with that lunatic and not him?

The fear of it, even though it hadn't happened, would never happen, kept Blake awake until the sun edged its way above the horizon.

# CHAPTER 23

Every morning of the next few days was the same. Every night, too. Kate would wake to kisses instead of the alarm clock buzzing and every night she'd fall asleep in Blake's arms. Tonight was Thursday. Tomorrow Friday and then Saturday, when they'd set the trap for Luke. Kate still didn't know if her hitching a ride from Eugene to Cottage Grove would be enough of a lure for him or not, but she was willing to try. They'd practiced what she was supposed to say to get him to talk about his plans. So that the wire she would have hidden on her body could send the conversation to the people listening, which was basically everyone: Sally, the police, the girls, Blake and her mom.

"Hey, darlin'." Blake looked up from reading the paper, feeling fine that he knew what it said this time.

"Hi." Kate smiled as she walked in the door from work. She set her bag down next to the desk. "I saw Sally. She said she'll come over in about an hour and bring Mom."

"Did you have a good day?" Blake asked as he pulled her into a kiss.

Kate grinned against his mouth. "Yes." She wound her arms around his neck. "You know, Sally put a tracking device on me. Do you want to find it?"

"No, she didn't." Blake molded her body to his. "That's why she's coming over. She wants us to understand how it works."

"Maybe you'd better look anyway." Kate lifted her shirt.

"You're getting cute, are you?" Blake asked as he grabbed Kate's waist and picked her up.

Before he could react, Kate wrapped her arms around his neck and her legs around his waist. She pressed her lips to his and slipped her tongue along his lips. Laughing, she reached deeper and wrapped her arms tighter around him. A shock ran through

Blake as if a lightning bolt had struck. The kiss that began as playful turned to burning desire. Warmth like fire burned his skin. His arms banded around Kate's slim body. Her curves molded to his hands. In just a few days he'd come to know her body well. He knew what his touch did to her. Hearing the soft purring coming from her throat, he smiled. He knew his fingers tracing the skin on her back did that. He closed his eyes against his hazy vision and pushed deeper into the kiss. A low moan filled with aching desire was heard and Blake knew it was his own.

Kate squirmed closer to his heat and twirled her fingers through his hair. Her want quickly turned to need and she tightened her legs around him. She loved the power she'd found. Loved it that he couldn't keep his hands off her. She knew that if she moved her tongue along his neck, up to his jaw, they'd be in the bed in a second. Grinning, Kate kissed the edge of his mouth and moved lower to the base of his throat.

It would be so easy to just sink to the floor, Blake thought. It would be so nice to see Kate's hair pool around her face and feel her soft breath caress his body like a warm summer breeze.

"What the hell?" Erin yelled as she and the girls in the house. "Can't you guys think of something else?" She laughed.

"Go away." Blake kissed Kate again.

"You're early." Kate smiled and shimmied down Blake to the floor.

"We thought we'd come by to see if you needed help making dinner," Ranae added with a smile.

"Dinner? I forgot," Kate said, mentally going over what was in the kitchen. "I didn't go shopping."

"What a surprise." Nichole's eyes shined. "So I brought stuff for hamburgers. We can grill."

"Great." Blake nodded, wishing they'd just go away. "I'll go start the charcoal."

Kate giggled as she watched him walk out of the house with a bent, dejected look.

"How you guys doing?" Erin asked. "And don't say, 'we're fine' in your sweet voice. I want to know the dirt."

"Yeah. We want to know everything." Nichole began slicing tomatoes.

Ranae set out the plates and pulled out the silverware for the table. "Is he romantic?"

Kate nodded and laughed. "He gives me a present every night."

"I'll bet," Erin said.

"Quit." Ranae elbowed Erin with her cast arm.

"Ouch. Stop doing that."

"Well, stop being a creep." Ranae laughed.

"What are the presents?" Nichole asked.

"Well," Kate said as she mixed the ground beef and spices. "The first gift was post cards from Alaska. He'd written little poems on the back. Then he gave me toenail polish and painted my toes. Last night he gave me those little pots of modeling clay and we made flowers and stars and stuff. It was really fun."

"God, what a sap." Erin rolled her eyes.

"I know. I love it." Nichole clasped her hands and jumped in place.

"I didn't know it could be so cool." Ranae swiped at the tears on her face. "I mean for real. He really loves you and it's good."

"Nae? Don't cry." Kate wrapped her arms around her. "Yeah, it's good."

"Uh-oh." Blake paused when he came in the door. "What's wrong?"

"Nothing. Nae's just sad 'cause you're so cool," Nichole teased.

"What?" Blake asked.

"No. She's happy because you make Kate happy." Erin smiled.

\*

Maggie could smell the hamburgers first thing and knew it was Kate who made them. When Kate was growing up, they were her favorite thing to eat. She worked out the recipe until they were perfect. The onion and garlic mixture sounded horrid, but the taste was wonderful.

"Mama!" Kate cried as she ran across the room. "I made hamburgers."

"I know. I can smell them," Maggie smiled. "Sally brought some lemonade and I brought rhubarb pie."

"Great. The treadmill's my best friend." Nichole smiled.

"Let's eat," Erin hollered from the kitchen.

Blake smiled at everyone sitting around the table. He truly loved being, and feeling, a part of this family. He'd planned to wait until tonight to give Kate her evening gift, but it was something that would affect all of them.

"Kate," Blake said. "I want to give you your gift now if that's okay."

Kate looked at him. He looked really serious. "Okay." She smiled. "If you want."

Blake handed her a small, silver cardboard box.

"It's heavy." Kate opened it and looked inside. "It's dirt? You're giving me dirt as a present?" Kate laughed.

"Yes it's dirt. But it's your dirt."

"Great. I always wanted some. I know just where I'm going to put it." Kate mimed dumping it on top of Blake's head as she snickered. "Wait though. What do you mean by *my* dirt."

"Do you remember at the rodeo in Wyoming where I wanted to talk to you?"

Kate nodded. It seemed like a lifetime ago.

"This is what I wanted to talk to you about."

"I don't understand."

"The dirt is from Montana."

"You're giving me dirt from Montana. Why?"

"Because we own a ranch there or we will." Blake hurried on. "I'm buying us one. I knew you'd want to hear about what it's like before I sign the papers. I thought the paperwork would take longer, but the real estate agent says we're all ready to go."

"You're buying a ranch—in Montana?" Kate stared at the dirt in the little silver box. "This is dirt from Montana?"

"Yes, Darlin'," Blake replied hoping that her shock would eventually turn to happiness. "I'm sorry I didn't tell you about it before, but I wanted it to be a surprise. But if you want, we can go look at it before I make it final. And, if you don't like it we can look for something else."

Blake's voice grew strained.

"I don't know what to say." Kate truly didn't. Could it be true? Would the sun really rise on their own land? Would she be able to ride Little Lady across the hills of Montana?

"Kate, I promise if you don't like it—" Blake stopped when he saw tears glisten on Kate's cheek. "Oh, Darlin'. I'm sorry. I wanted—"

"Blake," Kate whispered. "Don't be sorry."

"You're not upset?"

Kate replaced the lid to the box of dirt. "Of course I'm not upset. What's it like?"

"Well, let's see." Blake paused trying to figure out what Kate would want to know first. He smiled at his own nervousness. Telling her about the ranch was easy; all he had to do was start with the land. She loved it as he did. "The land has rolling green hills that meet the edge of the Bitterroot Mountain Range. A river winds its way through the property. The pasture land can sustain about two hundred cow/calf pairs."

"Oh my God!" Kate exclaimed.

"Yes, we'll have our work cut out for us. But I think I have a good man that can work as foreman. Anyway," Blake continued, "the outbuildings include a chicken coup, calving barn, hay shed, storage for tractors and sprinkler system machinery. The house is white and has two stories with an attic that the previous owners turned into a studio for painting and other art type stuff."

At that Kate smiled.

"Yes, I know," Blake said. "Photographs, you're thinking. Well, that's fine with me. There's a lot to take pictures of.

"How do you know about that?"

"Do you think I'm blind? You were crazy with a camera in the morning at the rodeos. You took pictures of the buckin' chutes at so many different angles in the sunrise, I thought I'd scream. Then I'd look at them when they were developed and feel like a fool, 'cause they were really good."

"Thanks."

"I thought you'd like the attic, but I also thought I'd tell you about the arena."

"Arena?" Kate couldn't contain the excitement. "Really! What's it like? Is it fenced? Does it have good dirt? Do we need to...sorry. You tell me."

"Yes, it has great dirt. I checked it myself. In fact, you're holding some of it."

Kate looked at the little box she held and felt a swish of excitement pour through her.

"Yes, the arena is fenced. It's fenced so well that it's indoors and you have an entire stable area running the entire length of it on the right side." Blake stopped. "Kate, darlin', what's the matter."

Kate shook her head. "Nothing."

"Tell me." Blake took the box of dirt and placed it on the table.

Kate looked up into Blake's blue eyes. "I don't know what to say. This is my dream. You made my dream come true."

"It's my dream, too. I do need a place to keep my cow horse, after all." Blake held Kate's face in his hands. "If you want to look for another place together, we can do that. We're partners in this."

"I don't want another place. I love that place this second like I picked it out myself. It's just hard to believe. I don't even know what to do."

"You can say thank you, Dolly," Maggie said as tears rolled down her own cheeks. Blake hadn't mentioned marriage, but he'd already asked her permission to propose to Kate.

"Thank you, Blake." Kate smiled.

"Now kiss him." Erin said and laughter erupted around the table. "This is so damn cool."

Nichole leaned over to Ranae who was crying for the second time that day. "It's good isn't it?"

"Yeah," she whispered. "It's good. It's just what I need."

*

It didn't take Sally long to show everyone how the system worked that would track Kate on Saturday. A device was hidden in a pair of tennis shoes that she would wear and her movements could be seen on a small screen. Kate walked around the house and everyone inside could see her steps. The wire that would transmit Kate's conversation with Luke was hidden in a pair of earrings that Sally fastened to Kate's ears. They were simple silver and gold wrapped studs. As soon as she saw Luke, Kate was directed to press her left earring. That would alert Sally that he was near and she could begin listening and recording their conversation. The plan was that as soon as Luke pulled over to pick Kate up, the police would move in and arrest him; it was up to Kate to keep him there long enough for that to be accomplished. Everything was to be public and as safe as possible.

Blake still hated the idea. As he waited for Kate to finish grading her final summer school papers, he mulled it over. Maybe he could just take Kate to the Caribbean or something until Luke was caught. He didn't want to put their life together on hold, but there had to be something. Something different.

# CHAPTER 24

"Good morning, Darlin'." Blake kissed Kate's sleepy eyes.

"Morning." Kate smiled, trying to clear her foggy mind. "What time is it?"

"Early. Like five."

"What's the matter?" Kate sat up.

"Nothing, I just wanted you." Blake kissed her long and deep until he felt her body respond beneath him. "You came to bed so late last night. I wanted you to sleep." He smiled.

"That was sweet of you, but come here." Kate wrapped her legs around him and kissed him back.

Tongues met tongues in an urgency that spoke of need. Fingers laced and pulled in passion. The control he'd kept such a tight rein on snapped. He wanted her. With the all the fire he had in him, he wanted to brand her as his own.

He rolled with her, not slowing his hands as they worked to have all of her. His mouth followed his hands. His tongue, his lips covered her breast. He felt her harden instantly beneath the cotton gown she wore.

She bowed beneath him with the pleasure of sweet agony. Power, the true power of womanhood shot through her veins as she matched his longing with hers. She twisted with the euphoria of the moment.

He tugged and tore at her gown until it ripped aside showing her glistening body as wet as the morning mist. He groaned and dove with her.

Their lips, their teeth met in reckless need.

This wasn't the gentle boy or the tempted girl from before. This was man and woman steeped in primal movement, drenched in sensation and glorying in it.

As the first shudder of painful ecstasy soared through her body, Kate screamed his name.

All he wanted was more. More of everything. He pushed her harder and faster. He wanted to keep her at that peak so he could join her. He wanted to keep the taste of her on his lips. Every time he felt her body tremor, he wanted her to do it again and again.

She could take no more and wanted him inside her. She opened and begged him to enter. He pulled her beneath him and saw her face, her tumbled hair in a blaze of burning steam. He plunged into the fire she offered. Scorching flames burned around them branding them both. Her as his. Him as hers.

"I'm never going to be able to move again." Blake gently kissed Kate's face and saw her smile. "I didn't hurt you, did I?" He thought for first time that he might've.

"No." She grinned. "Did I hurt you?"

"No." Blake felt for the little box that sat on the bed stand. He wanted to do this now, in the new light of the morning. He wanted to see the sunrise in her eyes as he asked her. "Kate." He paused and slipped the ring from the box. "I wanted this to be different. I wanted us to go back to that little town on the Kansas border where we met and spend the day walking and remembering. But I don't want to wait anymore. I may have fallen in love with that girl, but it is this woman before me that my heart wants the most. Will you be my wife?"

"What?" Kate looked into his eyes and then at the beautiful diamond in his hand. Tears began to fall. "I love you so much."

"I love you too, darlin'." He smiled and moved to put the ring on her finger, anxious to see it there.

"But I can't marry you."

"Why?"

"Because of Luke—"

"To hell with Luke. I love you and I want you to be my wife!" Blake yelled. All the anger, fear and frustration he'd been feeling came out in every word he said.

"I can't believe how stupid I was." Kate stood and put on her robe.

"What do you mean?" Blake asked, feeling his heart crack.

"When Luke's finished with me, he'll kill everyone I love." Kate pointed to the ring. "If I have that on my finger, he'll find you. Do you think I want you dead, too?" Kate yelled back and wiped her tears.

"Come here." Blake reached for her.

Kate shook her head. "No. This has just been a great dream. A dream that has to end." She looked at him.

The desperate longing in her eyes tore at his heart.

"Blake, I want you to promise me something."

"What?"

"I want you to promise that tonight when I come home from school, the girls will be gone and that you will be, too. I think Sally can take care of Mom, but I want you to take care of the girls."

"I can't do that. I can't leave." Blake grabbed a hold of Kate's arms. "How can you even ask me to do it?"

"Because I love you." Kate pushed him back. "Because I love them." She ran out of the room, sobbing.

"Damn it, Kate!" Blake yelled.

*

Kate had just a few more things to pack up from her classroom and one last box to carry to her car. The kids had helped throughout the day. They laughed and teased and had a great time filling the trunk with her things. The two short weeks of summer school were over. She looked around her room one last time. The walls were bare, the counters washed and the final box was waiting on her desk. She felt like her life was over. She knew it was. It was everything she could do not to just sit in the corner and cry.

"Feeling just a bit sad?" questioned a voice from the doorway.

"Yes, a little." Kate turned to face Coleen. "I loved my time here. The kids were great, the school, you were great. I'll miss you."

"Hey, you'll see me in a month or so. August will be here before you know it."

"Do you think I made a difference?" Do you think anyone will remember that I even was a teacher? I was only here for two weeks. Will they even remember my name by October?

"All teachers make a difference." Coleen looked at Kate. The last day of any school was difficult, but she couldn't figure out why Kate was being so sad. "But I think that you have touched many lives. You love what you teach. The kids see that. They also see that you are a bit of dreamer. That inspires them. They won't forget you and will be glad to see you in the Fall, if you decide to come back."

"Thank you." Kate walked to hug Coleen. "I haven't signed my contract, yet." Kate didn't want to feel committed to something she'd might never be able to do.

"I hope you will." Coleen hugged back, feeling very proud that she was able to spend some of her life, teaching and learning from a girl like Kate. "Now, there are some others who want to say good bye." Coleen stepped back and behind her was Kate's entire class.

Kate smiled and tried hard not to cry. "Hello, Ladies and Gentlemen," she said, using the greeting she always did.

"Hello, Miss White," the class called back, the same they always did.

Then they laughed, all of them. *I'm seeing the magic some teachers wait years to see*, Kate thought as she circled through the group giving hugs and shaking hands of the older boys who didn't believe in hugging a teacher, but then smiling all the more when they whipped their arms around her. "I love you, all," Kate cried. "Oh, I will miss you!"

"We'll miss you too," they called back.

"But we'll see you when school starts, won't we?" Andrew called.

"Yeah, my mom's excited that I know who Shakespeare is." Ryan laughed.

Jessie twirled. "I get to wear my new dress on the first day of school. I want you to see it."

"I'm going to spend a week with my grandma at the ocean, so I'll have new shells to show you," Candy said as she jumped up and down.

Kate laughed and laughed through all of the proclamations. Still surrounded by her students, she grabbed the last box to head out to the car. She didn't want to stand and say good-bye to a place she'd only had for a short time. She didn't want to focus on the misery she felt as she left. She just wanted to move on to tomorrow and get it over with.

"Oh, I'll take that Miss White," Andrew said as he held out his arms.

"Okay, thanks." Kate handed him the box and patted his head as she had done many times before. Secretly, she had hoped that if she ever had a son, he would be as wonderful as Andrew. Kate fought back the tears that threatened. She'd never have a son.

"Well, it looks like they're going to walk you out," called Coleen who had come to stand in the doorway of her room.

"I guess so. I'll send them back your way and on home when I get to the car."

"Great, call if you need anything."

Once outside, Andrew raced to the car parked in the shade near the edge of the teacher parking lot and put the box in the trunk. By the time Kate called to all the kids, telling them good-bye and to go home, Andrew was racing into Kate's arms.

"I love you, Miss White," Andrew whispered.

"Oh, honey, I love you, too."

"You're not coming back, are you?"

"I don't know. But I'll think of you all of the time. Remember that sketching paper I gave you?"

"Yes."

"Well, whenever you write or draw on it, remember I'm thinking of you. Okay?"

"I will."

Kate stepped back and saw tears in the little boy's eyes. He was at the edge of childhood and had already had to deal with what it was to be a man. "You are stronger than you think. You'll have a great future." Kate tapped his nose with her finger.

"I don't think it's really fair."

"What's not fair?"

"That I have to lose two moms in the same lifetime."

"You're not losing me. I'll be here for a while. Maybe you can come visit. There's a rodeo coming up, maybe—"

"Really. Do you think they'd let me ride a horse or a bull even?" The little boy was back and the tears were drying in the breeze.

"A horse definitely, but the bull—I don't know what your dad thinks about that."

"Oh, he won't care. He wanted to be a bull rider before he had me. He might still. He's young enough."

Kate nodded thinking how sad it was for a man who was just a few years older than her to have to face raising a child alone. But she smiled as she reached for the car handle and watched as Andrew galloped around in a circle with his hand reaching for the sky like a bull rider would. Opening the door, she heard a voice.

"Hello, Kate."

Kate glanced quickly at Andrew, who seemed to know instantly that something had changed and was running to her side.

"Andrew, I want to you go inside."

"Okay." He looked passed her shoulder to see a man stab a knife through the red skin of an apple. It was the apple he had given Miss White. Andrew knew it because he could see the little heart note dangling from the stem. "Who's that?"

"This is Luke. He's a friend of mine. He came to meet me today." Kate tried desperately to keep the fear from her voice.

"How come you've never mentioned him?"

"Well, I didn't know he was coming. Honey, I want you to go back inside." Kate tried to smile.

"Okay." Andrew hugged her one last time. "I'll see you at the rodeo," he called, knowing exactly who he was going to go see once he was inside the school. He was going to go tell Mrs. O'Konel that there was a strange man in a suit sitting in Miss White's car and that Miss White was scared. Then they were going to call the police. His father was the sheriff, and he would know what to do.

# CHAPTER 25

"You never answered me, Kate. I said hello."

"Hello, Luke." Kate forced herself to answer. She had to force herself to look at him. In reality it had been a long time since she'd seen him. In her mind she saw him almost daily. Looking at him now was strange. She didn't expect to see what she saw. In her memory he was a monster in a fine suit. The person sitting in the passenger seat of her car was a mere shadow. The suit he wore was elegant, but it draped from his shoulders. His face was a sweaty pale. The skin around his eyes was sunken and dark. As Kate looked, she almost felt sorry for him. His anger and rage had withered him. His eyes though, were the same: searching, hatred filled. Looking into to them, Kate shuddered.

"Did you miss me?"

Hearing his voice brought the memory of the night she had worked so hard to forget. Tears formed in her eyes as panic filled her. She had to beat it back. She had to blink away the fear. "How did you find me?"

"I remembered you talking about your mother living in Oregon. When you weren't in Colorado any more, I thought I'd look here."

"What do you want?"

"I'll tell it to you while you drive."

"Where do you want to go?" Kate looked around trying to gauge whether she could run and how far she would get.

"Get in."

"And if I don't."

"Do you see those kids?" Luke pointed the knife tip toward the playground.

"You will not hurt them. They have nothing to do with this."

"Oh, yeah, we'll see." Luke twirled the blade in small circles on his finger. "They can die, too."

"No," Kate yelled and then cursed herself for her stupidity as her voice carried across the parking lot to the playground where some of her students were playing.

"Let's see who's first." Luke's laugh drifted threateningly outward as the students ran toward Kate.

"Go home. I'll see you soon!" She yelled as she jumped into the car. "You will burn in hell if you hurt my kids." Kate started her car and threw it into reverse. When she looked in the rearview mirror she saw the earrings Sally had pinned in her ears last night. Quickly, she pressed her left ear and waved to the kids. As she pulled out of the school parking lot away from them, leaving confused looks on their faces, she felt relieved that they hadn't made it to the car.

"Always the protector aren't you, Kate? But who's going to protect you from me?"

"What do you want, Luke?" Kate's mind was racing trying to think of ways to keep him talking. She needed time to think about how to get away from him and a way to let Sally know where she was. She needed to keep the fear she felt from taking over, because she didn't know if Sally was even aware that she was needed.

"I want you. I want you dreaming of me."

That statement had brought so much terror to Kate's life. Her hands trembled with the fear of it. She felt like she was in her dream. But this was real. The pain would be real. The blood. The death. She didn't know if she could escape this time.

"Do you know where the run down mill is out of town?" Luke asked.

"I think so." Kate kept telling herself not to be afraid, but her body shook.

"Go there."

"Why?"

"Didn't you get my letter?" He was feeling better. She looked scared. But she'd still fight. It would be good.

"What letter?" asked Kate pretending she didn't know what was going on. That would keep him asking questions at least and maybe he'd slip up.

"Stupid cops!"

*Think, Kate. Think.* She wanted to confuse him. Make him angry so she could get away. "I got one rose, months ago. I just assumed it was from my fiancé. I don't think about you anymore." Kate thought maybe that was too much. She glanced Luke's way. His eyes held cold fury. She didn't have any time to duck or even blink. Luke's fist slammed into her face. Her head whipped back. Blood gushed from her nose.

The car swerved. Kate's eyes stung with pain, but she held it together enough to right the car back to its own lane.

"Remember me now, you bitch?" Luke yelled.

Kate held her nose. Trying to stop the blood that cooled against her skin. "What do you have in mind?"

"Don't you remember?"

"No, Luke, why don't you tell me?" Kate was tired of the sick, scared feeling she'd had in the pit of her stomach for days. When she felt his fist slam into her and the hot blood spurt out, fear went away. It was replaced with a fury of her own. She wanted to fight now. "Tell me so I can remember what it was like. Did you miss me, Luke?" He had no right to do what he was doing. He had no right to take her life away. He was not going to, either.

"Luke, tell me how you got here?" Kate asked not sure where he'd gone.

"I came in a car."

"Whose car?" Kate gripped the steering wheel. Her knuckles turned marble white.

"I don't know her name."

"Did you kill her, Luke?"

"Of course I did." Luke laughed. "As if you have to ask. Her body is still warm with blood flowing from her veins in that mill up there."

Kate saw the mill and the train tracks that crossed the road in front of them. Wide, tall brick buildings guarded the empty acreage around them. Silver sided sheds glinted in the sunlit afternoon. Trees grew, sad and overgrown at the edges. Her stomach clenched. This was her way home. This was her one chance. The light in front of her was flashing yellow, when it turned to red, Kate would drive across the tracks.

"Why did you do it?" Kate asked.

"She deserved it. Like you do."

"Like your mom did." Kate hoped Luke wouldn't figure out what she was doing. For an instant, she thought he did when his knife made a slash up her leg slicing into her skin. Kate grimaced and sucked in a breath. She could wait. She would not let her fear win. He was crazy. She was going to use it. She drove her car across the first set of railroad tracks and stopped. One set of tracks went west the other went east. The first train from the east would come in the next few seconds. Then the train from the west would come. It would be loud. Kate knew.

She had to wait for them every day, unless she left early. Her car was sitting directly across the tracks from the west. There would be only a few moments of time for Kate to escape. If she could keep him talking, she could use those few *precious* moments.

"What did you do to your mom, Luke?"

"Exactly what she deserved. Just like your little friend. She died screaming in that fire."

"No, she didn't. She didn't die in that fire."

"What are you talking about, you bi—" His words were drowned out by the blast of a train horn. The train whipped the car with the wind it created, passing within only a few feet.

Kate held her breath and looked quickly to the west. Here it comes. Just a bit longer. Just a bit. The seconds paused.

Luke swore, "Start the car, you bitch." He held the knife to her throat.

She fumbled with the ignition. She turned the key, but it wouldn't start. She'd stalled it, flooded it on purpose. All she was doing was killing seconds. Her heart pounded as she pumped the gas pedal and tried the key.

Tears stung her eyes. The girls were waiting. Her life waited—Blake waited. Kate took hold of the silver door handle. The cold of it didn't register. She gripped it with her hand. She squeezed her eyes. Took a deep breath. All that she wished for flew through her mind, her own children learning to ride their first horse, white Christmases in Montana, barrel racing, rodeo, dancing with her husband—dancing with Blake. Kate opened her eyes. *I have to live.* The train got closer and closer. The huge locomotive grew. Its light blared. She could smell the stifling heat. Hear the bellowing horn.

Kate pushed at Luke with all her strength. She flew from the car. And ran. She heard his scream of terror. She tripped, but never stopped. Never. She would never stop fighting. Crawling on the ground, scrambling to her knees, to her feet, she ran toward the woods. Her lungs were stinging, on fire. Turning she saw the terrified Luke strike and struggle against the passenger door. She turned to run again. The train exploded against the car. The force of its wind smashed against Kate. She stumbled, lost her balance and slammed to the ground. Her eyes went blank. She saw only black.

*

Sirens wailed to the scene. The firemen and Andrew's dad, the sheriff, worked as a team, calling orders and carrying them out. Soon foam from the long fire hose arched high and fast through the air, pushing at the smoke and flames.

The girls scrambled out of Leona's Cadillac, running and calling. Blake ran towards the burning car. Sally grabbed him, holding him back. Blake tore at her and tried to get to Kate's car.

"No, damn it. Kate's smarter than that," Sally screamed.

"What if she's in there?"

"She's not. She can't be. Where is she!"

"Kate!" Blake yelled, screamed. Fear had never gripped him like this—hot tears burned his face. Flames rose to the sky in heated black smoke. "Kate, answer me! Kate, God, please! I can't live without you. You answer me!" Blake would have gladly run into those flames.

"Blake!" Nichole screamed above his fear.

Turning, Blake saw the girls. They were huddled several hundred yards from the burning car. Hope slammed into his chest as he ran to them. Falling to his knees he scooped Kate into his arms. He cradled her face in his hands.

"Darlin'?" he whispered.

"Maybe we shouldn't move her." Nichole stepped forward.

"She might be hurt," Erin said.

Blake didn't hear them. He was furious with himself. Would he never be there when Kate needed him? He was supposed to be. He wanted to be. If he had been, she wouldn't be here. Her clothes and her face wouldn't be bloody. Her eye wouldn't already be darkening with a swelling bruise.

"Wake up." He brushed his fingers along her cheek. Feeling relief when Kate's eyes fluttered open.

Kate woke to warm arms clutching her. She knew who it was. Lifting her eyes she saw him.

"Are you hurt?"

"Not anymore." Kate smiled.

"Are you sure?"

"Blake," she whispered.

"Yeah, darlin'?"

"He's gone, Blake." Kate looked into Blake's blue eyes, showing him relief and love. A tear formed and slipped to his cheek. She reached with her thumb and pressed it away. "He's gone."

"I know. I can't talk. Just let me hold you." Wrapping his arms tighter, Blake swore he would never again let her fight alone.

The world held the last warmth of the day as the sun shown in a misty sheen all around them. Her friends stood, holding on to each other and kneeling beside her. Sally and her mom stood beside them.

"Blake?"

"Yeah, darlin'?"

"Do you still have the ring?"

He nodded and pulled it out of his pocket. "My heart sure wants you to wear it."

"My heart wants it, too." Kate smiled as he slipped the ring on her finger. "My heart wants it, too."

# About the Author

Growing up out West, Rionna Morgan followed her love of horses to the rodeo arena and her love of English to teaching and to writing. She has been looking forward to sharing her stories with you her whole life. Rionna is a founding member of Montana Romance Writers; she reads as much as she can possibly hold, and she loves most of all the chilling thrill of great a suspense threaded through a great romance. Rionna shares her home in Missoula, Montana with her husband, her four children and the mountains outside her window. You can visit her at rionnamorgan.com. Please do—she loves the company.

*

www.ingramcontent.com/pod-product-compliance
Lightning Source LLC
Chambersburg PA
CBHW010638100726
47900CB00011B/2877